The Earth Turned Upside Down

The Earth Turned Upside Down

Jules Verne

Translated by Sophie Lewis

Published by Hesperus Press Limited
28 Mortimer Street, London W1W 7RD
www.hesperuspress.com

The Earth Turned Upside Down first published by Hesperus Press, 2012

First published in French as *Sans dessus dessous* in 1889

English language translation © Sophie Lewis, 2012
Foreword © Ian Fells, 2012

Designed and typeset by Fraser Muggeridge studio
Printed in Jordan by Jordan National Press

ISBN: 978-1-84391-367-2

CONTENTS

FOREWORD

Jules Verne, with his science-based adventure stories, was at the height of his powers and reputation when he wrote *Sans dessus dessous*, titled, in this translation, *The Earth Turned Upside Down*, in 1889. He had written about space, air and underwater travel in *Twenty Thousand Leagues under the Sea*, *From the Earth to the Moon*, *Journey to the Centre of the Earth* and *Around the World in Eighty Days*; they were known collectively as *Les Voyages Extraordinaires*. Here, in *The Earth Turned Upside Down*, he ventures into what is known, fashionably in 2012, as geoengineering. This latest book is almost frightening in its prescience, following *From the Earth to the Moon*, in which three members of the Gun Club of Baltimore were fired from a giant cannon, circled the moon and returned to splash down in the sea in an aluminium capsule. (This anticipated the American landing on the moon by almost a hundred years.) In *The Earth Turned Upside Down*, The Gun Club members, led by Mr J-T Maston, propose to use the same idea of a giant cannon, aided by Newton's Laws of Motion, to spin the earth in such a way that it would tilt on its axis and the North Pole would be moved to the 67th parallel and enjoy temperate weather; the ice would melt and make accessible extensive coal seams. There was concern in the late nineteenth century that coal reserves might move into short supply; this worry is still with us today with the fear that both world oil and coal supplies have peaked.

Impey Barbicane, president of the Baltimore Gun Club, proposes that The North Polar Exploitation Association be set up for the purpose of auctioning the land between 84 degrees north and the North Pole, comprising an area one tenth that of Europe, to the highest bidder. The lucky winner could thus accrue enormous wealth by exploiting the coal. Of course finance is required and Mr Maston is fortunate in having an admirer, Mrs Evangelina Scorbitt, a wealthy American widow, to provide funds for the venture. And so the Americans beat off the Europeans to buy the North Pole and surrounding 407,000 square miles (at 200 cents per square mile), and the North Polar Exploitation Association readies itself for the great experiment.

Jules Verne captures the tremendous confidence of the Victorian entrepreneurs. In Great Britain there were Armstrong, Parsons, Swan, and George and Robert Stephenson. They transformed power generation, armaments, lighting and travel. In France, Eiffel built his spectacular tower in Paris and many impressive bridges. In America, Thomas Edison invented the phonograph and, independently from Swan, the incandescent electric light bulb; Alexander Graham Bell invented the telephone and initiated the communication explosion. They were men of enormous imagination and also men of action. They did not go cap-in-hand to governments for grants to support their work; they got on, raised the money by public subscription and made, and lost, fortunes.

Verne had already written *Paris in the Twentieth Century* (1863), an account of a young man who lives in a world of glass skyscrapers, high-speed trains, calculators and a worldwide communication network. There was universal enthusiasm for science and technology. The World Fair was held in Paris in 1889 and Jules Verne then turned his hand to the perceived impending world shortage of coal but, more importantly, to making money. In *The Earth Turned Upside Down*, Impey Barbicane, Captain Nicholl and J-T Maston, the stalwarts of the Baltimore Gun Club, stand to make a great deal of money from their venture. However, their enormous enthusiasm for the project causes them to ride roughshod over the attendant dangers of their experiment in geoengineering: the possibility of huge sea level changes as a result of the effects of the huge explosion of the cannon, primed with the new explosive 'dyna-mix', and the resulting destabilizing effect on the world's climate.

Today, in the twenty-first century, over a hundred years later, we are only just discussing geoengineering possibilities, such as pouring huge amounts of finely divided iron into the South Pacific to stimulate a gigantic algal bloom, which would mop up carbon dioxide and postpone global warming. Or putting thousands of satellites into geostationary orbit to capture the sun's rays, convert them into electricity and beam the energy down to earth as microwaves. We could tap into heat from the centre of the earth, or collect energy from the great water flows in the sea, such as the Gulf Stream, where five cubic miles of water flow past the tip of Florida every second. But would such a venture change the circulation pattern of water in the Atlantic Ocean and would Great Britain finish up with a climate much the same as St Petersburg? Some of these propositions would have been grist to Verne's mill.

It is tempting to speculate as to what Jules Verne would turn his hand to today if he were still writing science fiction. The genre has moved on into strange territory, stimulated by the prospect of lucrative film and television rights. His own nineteenth-century books and writings have been made into outstanding films; *Round the World in Eighty Days* was a great success. But would he have ventured into the world of aliens, wars amongst the stars as H.G. Wells did, or into the dark worlds of magic and evil, with the violent overtones of today's science fiction? The internet would have excited his imagination with its explosion of information storage and retrieval. But his work was predicated on nineteenth-century hunger for things scientific or technological. He would have ample scope with topics such as dark matter, nanotechnology, genetic engineering, manipulation of the weather machine and new ways of generating electricity (perhaps 'cold fusion' would have grabbed his attention). Or would he have projected forward to a time when we can control gravity and harness the unbelievable gravitational fields which surround black holes? A Gravity Amplifier would make space travel more possible; even something approaching a perpetual motion machine could be envisaged. The laws of physics are under threat with suggestions that Einstein might be wrong with his insistence on the immutable speed of light, and what of the Higgs Boson?

Had the proposal to change the tilt of the earth in favour of the North Pole so that it would have a temperate climate succeeded, the investors in the company would have been disappointed. There are no coal seams under the North Pole. However a consequence of the monumental change in the world's tilt would also have been to make Antarctica a temperate region as well as the Arctic and it is now known that coal and other minerals are present in abundance underneath the South Pole.

The twists and turns of the story as Jules Verne tells it are fascinating; they involve greed, hubris, arrogance, errors in calculation and love. The tale bears a number of morals for our time.

Logic will get you from A to B but imagination will take you everywhere – Albert Einstein.

– Professor Ian Fells, 2012

The Earth Turned
Upside Down

I

'So, Mr Maston, you claim that women were incapable of ever advancing either the mathematical or the experimental sciences?'

'I'm afraid that is what I am forced to think, Mrs Scorbitt,' said J-T Maston. 'It's certainly the case that there have been, and even are now, a few astonishing lady mathematicians, particularly in Russia. But, with the type of brains females have, no woman could ever become an Archimedes or still less a Newton.'

'Oh, Mr Maston! I protest in the name of our sex...'

'A sex that is all the more delightful, Mrs Scorbitt, by virtue of its unsuitability for metaphysical studies.'

'So according to you, Mr Maston, on seeing an apple fall, no woman could have discovered the laws of gravity, as did the well-known seventeenth-century English scientist.'

'On seeing an apple fall, Mrs Scorbitt, a woman's only thought would be... to eat it. Thus following the example of our mother Eve!'

'Really? So you mean to deny that we have any aptitude for elevated thought...'

'*Any* aptitude? Not so, Mrs Scorbitt. And yet, I would point out that, since men have populated the Earth – and women too, as a result – no one has yet discovered a female brain equal to that of Aristotle, or Euclid or Kepler or Laplace, in the field of science.'

'So that's your whole argument, that the past must always determine the future?'

'I've no doubt that whatever has not happened in thousands of years will never happen…'

'Well, I shall have to take up our cause, Mr Maston, and we really are not good…'

'For anything but being good!' replied J-T Maston.

This was said with the all the gallantry of a scientist fairly drunk with Xs and Ys. And Mrs Evangelina Scorbitt was quite prepared to make do with it.

'Indeed Mr Maston!' She went on, 'To each his role in life. You have to be the extraordinary mathematician that you are and give yourself over to the problems presented by this immense project which occupies every waking moment for you and your friends. I shall be the "good woman" that is my role, and provide financial assistance…'

'For which we owe you our eternal gratitude,' replied J-T Maston.

Mrs Evangelina Scorbitt blushed delicately, for she felt – if not for all scientists, at least for J-T Maston – a truly unusual sympathy. The heart of a woman is not always easy to understand.

The project to which this rich American widow had resolved to donate substantial resources was truly immense. It covered the following Arctic territories:

According to Maltebrun, Reclus, Saint-Martin and the most authoritative geographers, the Arctic territories proper include:
1. Northern Devon, i.e. the ice-covered islands in Baffin Bay and the Lancaster Sound;
2. Northern Georgia, made up of the Banks region and a mass of islands, including the islands of Sabine, Byam-Martin, Griffith, Cornwallis and Bathurst;

3. The Baffin-Parry archipelago, including many sections of the circumpolar continent, among them: Cumberland, Southampton, James-Sommerset, Boothia-Felix, Melville, and others largely unknown.

Taken as a piece, the land encompassed by the 78th parallel extends over 1,400,000 square miles and the seas over 700,000 square miles.

Within this boundary, modern explorers have advanced right up to the edge of latitude 84°, discovering a number of coasts previously hidden behind the lofty chain of ice floes, naming the headlands, promontories, gulfs and bays of these vast lands, which we may call the Scottish Highlands of the Arctic. But beyond that 84th parallel, all is mystery, the unattainable focus of the cartographers' desire, and none can yet tell if, in that six-degree stretch, it is land or sea that is concealed by the impenetrable towers of ice at the northern Pole.

Now, in the year 1890, the government of the United States proposed, rather surprisingly, that the uncharted circumpolar regions be put up for auction – regions which an American society, recently formed for the purpose of securing the Arctic icecap, were looking to possess.

Some years ago, it is true, the Berlin Conference drew up a law to regulate those Great Powers which sought to appropriate the property of others in the name of colonisation or of the opening-up of new trade routes. Yet the law did not appear to apply in this case, since the polar region was entirely uninhabited. Nevertheless, since you could say that what belongs to nobody belongs equally to everybody, the newly formed society didn't seek to 'take' but to 'acquire' the land, in order to head off future objections.

In America, there is no project so audacious – or even plain impossible – that there aren't people who appreciate its practical aspects and provide funds to set it in motion. This was shown clearly a few years ago when the Baltimore Gun Club attempted to send a projectile to the Moon, in the hope of establishing direct communication with our satellite. It was Americans who provided the large sums to fund this interesting experiment. And two members of the Gun Club who took all the risks.

If a Count Lesseps, for example, should propose one day to dig a deep canal right across Europe and Asia, from the shores of the Atlantic through to the seas of China; if a well-digger should offer to drill down to the strata of silicates that lie in a liquid state above the molten iron, in order to draw heat from the very heart of our Earth's central fire; if an enterprising electrical engineer should wish to combine all the electric currents that are dispersed across the Earth's surface, and so create an inexhaustible source of light and heat; if a bold scientist should think of storing up the excess heat of our summers in vast receptacles, to release in the coldest area during the winter; if a hydraulics specialist should attempt to harness the power of the tides to produce either heat or energy; if societies or business partnerships be founded to bring to fruition a hundred projects of this sort – it is Americans who will be there, leading the subscriptions and raising the share capital, and rivers of dollars will flow into the communal coffers, just as the great rivers of North America are absorbed back into the deep oceans.

So it was of some concern to the general public when the surprise news broke that the Arctic was to be auctioned off to the highest bidder. What's more, there was no opportunity for the public to invest because the capital had already been raised. The actual use to be made of the Arctic was not to be revealed until it was in the possession of the new purchasers.

Exploiting the Arctic at all seemed a mad idea, on the basis of what was known about that barren area. And yet, no project could have been more serious.

Indeed, a letter was sent to the newspapers of all continents, to the European, African, Oceanian and Asiatic gazettes as well as to the American papers. It ended by calling for a survey of all the advantages and disadvantages on behalf of all interested parties. The *New York Herald* was first with this scoop. In the 7th November edition, Gordon Bennett's subscribers found the following announcement which then flew rapidly around the worlds of academia and commerce, to a mixed reception.

A Notice to all inhabitants of the Earth:

The regions of the North Pole, located within latitude 84° North, have not yet been exploited, since they have not yet been properly explored.

In fact, the furthest latitudes reached by explorers of different nationalities are the following:

82°45', reached by the Englishman William Parry in July 1847, on the 28th meridian West, North of Spitzberg;

83°20'28, reached by Albert Markham of Sir George Nares' English expedition of May 1876, at the 50th meridian West, North of Grinnell Land;

83°35', reached by Lockwood and Brainard, of Lieutenant Greely's American expedition in May 1882, on the 42nd meridian West, North of Nares Land.

We are therefore justified in treating the region that extends from the 84th parallel up to the Pole, for a distance of six degrees, as a territory jointly held in trust by the nations of the Earth, and available to be converted into private property, after a fair public sale.

According to the principles of the law, no property should be without an owner. Consequently, in accordance with these principles, the United States of America has resolved to supervise the reassignment of this region.

A society has been established in Baltimore, under the corporate title of the North Polar Exploitation Association, as the official representative of the United States. This society proposes to acquire the above-mentioned territory, under the appropriate legal conditions, along with absolute proprietorial rights over the continents, islands, islets, rocks, seas, lakes, rivers, streams and all other waterways in general, of which the Arctic is currently composed, whether or not they be covered with perpetual ice-floes, and whether or not they are freed of this ice during the summer season.

It is expressly stated that this proprietorial right may not be annulled, even in the event of modifications – whatever their nature – occurring in the geographical or meteorological state of the Earth.

This Notice being brought to the attention of the inhabitants of both Old and New Worlds, all states are invited to take part in the auction, and the property will then be awarded to the highest final bidder.

The auction will be held on the 3rd December this year in the Auction Rooms in Baltimore, Maryland, in the United States of America.

All further enquiries to William S. Forster, acting agent for the North Polar Exploitation Association, 93 High Street, Baltimore.

While the substance of this announcement might seem a piece of madness, it laid out its terms in clarity and directness. In any case, as a testimony of its seriousness, the American government had already granted the Arctic territories to the new society, in anticipation of an eventual owner buying it at auction.

But public opinion was divided. Some saw in it a typical example of American humbug, one which would break all previous records for self-promotion. Others thought that the proposition ought to be taken seriously. These pointed out that the new society was making no demands on the public's pockets, hoping instead to acquire these northern regions solely with its own funds. It was not looking to grab the dollars, banknotes, or gold and silver of any gullible members of the public to fill its coffers. It was merely asking to be allowed to purchase the circumpolar property with its own resources.

To lawyers, it seemed that the society need only plead the right of first occupant, then simply take possession of the land whose sale it was now encouraging. But there lay the problem, for, up to that day, no human had set foot on the Polar territories. Therefore, if the United States should try to sell this land, the buyer would require a watertight legal contract, so that nobody could later challenge the transaction. It would be unfair to blame either party for this. They were proceeding prudently and, when it comes to making commitments in an affair of this kind, one cannot take too many legal precautions.

Besides, the announcement included a clause guarding against unforeseeable future factors. This clause might give rise to a number of contradictory interpretations, for its precise meaning escaped even the subtlest minds. It was the last phrase, stipulating that 'this proprietorial right may not be annulled, even in the event that modifications – whatsoever their nature – occur in the geographical or meteorological state of the Earth.'

9

What could this sentence mean? What eventuality was it intended to anticipate? In what way might the Earth undergo a modification that would affect its geography or meteorology – particularly given the nature of the land put up for auction?

'Of course,' said the more astute, 'there must be something behind it!'

It was therefore a field day for competing interpretations, a fine occasion for some to exercise their perspicacity and others their curiosity.

First, the Philadelphia *Ledger* published this note: 'Their calculations have no doubt revealed to the future purchasers of the Arctic regions that a comet with a solid core is due to crash into the Earth and that its impact will produce the geographical and meteorological changes referred to in the clause.' The sentence clarified nothing. Moreover, serious thinkers dismissed the likelihood of a comet crashing like this. In any case, the American purchasers would never be concerned by such a hypothetical eventuality.

'Could it be, perhaps,' the New Orleans *Delta* wrote, 'that the new Society imagines the precession of the equinoxes might at some time produce alterations favourable to the development of its property?'

'And why not, since this movement affects the alignment of the earth's axis?' remarked the *Hamburger Correspondent*.

'Indeed,' responded the *Revue Scientifique* in Paris, 'did Adhémar not propose, in his volume on *The Revolutions of the Sea*, that the precession of the equinoxes combined with the centennial shifting of the Earth's orbit, would be sufficient to cause a long-term modification in the average temperature of different points on the Earth and in the quantities of ice accumulated at its two poles?'

'That is unconfirmed,' retorted the *Edinburgh Review*. 'And if it happened to be correct, wouldn't it take 12,000 years for Vega to become our pole star after the event, and therefore for the position of the Arctic territories to undergo climate change?'

'Well then,' replied the *Dagblad* in Copenhagen, 'in 12,000 years, it will be time to pour in the funds. But until that day, risk a *krone* on it – never!'

Still, while the *Revue Scientifique* may have been right about Adhémar, it was actually quite unlikely that the North Polar Exploration Association had ever relied on such an effect of equinoctial precession.

In fact, no one came up with a plausible meaning for the clause, with its hints of future cosmic alterations.

It might have been possible to find out more by approaching the new society's governing board and, more particularly, its president. But the president was unknown, as were the secretary and all the members of the board. No one even knew who had sent the letter. It had been brought to the offices of the *New York Herald* by a certain William S. Forster of Baltimore, a codfish trader for the firm of Ardrinell & Co., of Newfoundland – obviously a straw man. He was as silent on the subject as the goods sold in his shops, and so the most persuasive and inquisitive reporters could extract nothing from him. In short, this North Polar Exploration Association was so anonymous that no name could be connected with it. Which is indeed the ultimate anonymity.

Nevertheless, while the promoters of the project persisted in keeping their character veiled in mystery, their aim was exactly as stated in the announcement published worldwide.

As it happened, their aim was indeed to acquire sole ownership of the area covered by the Arctic regions, as demarcated by the 84th degree of latitude, which has the North Pole at its centre.

This was because, of the modern explorers, those who had come closest to this inaccessible spot – Parry, Markham, Lockwood and Brainard – had all stopped short of that parallel. In the area they chose to purchase, the North Polar Exploitation Association would impinge on no previous explorations. It was aiming for territory untouched by humankind.

It was a large area. From 84° to 90° is six degrees' distance, which, at sixty miles per degree, gives a radius of 360 miles and a diameter of 720 miles. So the circumference is 2,260 miles and the surface area about 407,000 square miles. That makes it about a tenth of the continent of Europe – a fair-sized plot.

The communiqué also put forward the idea that these regions, as yet unlabelled by geography, by not belonging to anyone belonged to everyone. The expectation was that the majority of the Great Powers would not dream of complaining about this. But for the states bordering the regions, there might be more at stake. They could consider the land an extension of their northern possessions and so might insist upon proprietorial rights. And anyway, their claims could be all the more justified since the discoveries made so far in the Arctic lands had been due specifically to the bravery of their countrymen. In view of this, the American government, as represented by the new society, advised them to submit their claims and promised to compensate them to the value of the acquisition. Nevertheless, the association's supporters continued to insist that the property was unallocated and so no one had a right to oppose the auctioning of the North Pole and its surroundings.

There were six states bordering on the Arctic whose rights were indisputable: America, England, Denmark, Sweden-Norway, Holland and Russia. In addition, some other states might also find reasons to put in a claim as a result of discoveries made by their own explorers.

So France could have staked a claim, several of her sons having taken part in expeditions to conquer the circumpolar territories. The courageous Bellot, for example, who died in 1853, in the region of Beechey Island, while on the campaign of the *Phénix*, in search of John Franklin. Then there was Doctor Octave Pavy, who died in 1884 close by Cape Sabine, during the Greely expedition's stop at Fort Conger. Not to mention the expedition of 1838–9 which took Charles Martins, Marmier, Bravais and their daring companions as far as the seas of Spitzberg. It would surely be unjust to consign them to oblivion. Despite this, France judged it inappropriate to get mixed up in this enterprise, which she viewed as more commercial than scientific, and she abandoned her slice of the polar cake, over which the other Great Powers stood to risk some broken teeth. Perhaps she was well-advised and made the right decision.

Germany decided similarly. Since 1671, she could cite the campaign to Spitsbergen led by Frederick Martens of Hamburg and, in 1869–70, the expeditions of the *Germania* and the *Hansa*, led by Koldervey and Hegeman, which travelled as far as Cape Bismarck, keeping to the Greenland coast. However, despite this history of brilliant discoveries, she did not feel in the least obliged to augment the German empire with a slice of the North Pole.

The same went for Austria-Hungary, despite her possession of the territories of Franz Josef Land, north of the Siberian littoral.

As for Italy, having no cause to join the battle, she did not join it – however unlikely that may seem.

There were of course also the Samoyeds of Asian Siberia, the Eskimos, who were particularly widespread across northern America, the inhabitants of Greenland, Labrador, the Baffin-Parry archipelago, the Aleutian Islands, clustered between Asia and America, and finally those who go by the name of Chukchi and live in formerly Russian Alaska but became American in 1867. But these peoples – all things considered, the true natives, the incontestable aboriginals of the northern regions – were not to be given a say in the matter. And besides, how could these poor peoples have managed to place a bid, however minimal, in the sale initiated by the North Polar Exploitation Association? How could they have made a payment? In shells, in walrus teeth, or in seal oil? Yet, it really belonged to them, by right of first occupancy, this territory that was up for auction. Unsurprisingly, Eskimos, Chukchis, Samoyeds and the rest were not even consulted.

That is how the world works.

II

IN WHICH THE READER MEETS
THE ENGLISH, DUTCH, SWEDISH,
DANISH AND RUSSIAN DELEGATES

The notice from the Association deserved a reply. Indeed, if the Association were to acquire the northern regions, they would definitively be made over to the United States, whose vigorous federation appeared to keep on expanding. Already, a few years ago, Russia's cession of the North-Western territories from the Northern Cordillera up to the Bering Strait, had appended a good portion of the New World to itself. It was understandable, then, that the other powers might not look favourably on the US annexation of the Arctic area.

Nevertheless, the various states of Europe and Asia – those without borders along the Arctic regions – refused to take part in this singular auction, so dubious did its likely outcome appear. Only those powers whose coasts lay near the 84th degree decided to participate by sending official delegates. And none of these states intended to bid more than a relatively modest price since even the eventual owner of the territory might never manage actually to take possession of it. Nevertheless, England, insatiable for new territories, felt obliged to provide her agent with a fairly substantial credit. It has to be said that the sale of the circumpolar lands in no way threatened European equilibrium, and no international complications were expected to arise. Mr Bismarck – the great chancellor being still alive at this time – kept his luxuriant brows, as of a Teutonic Jove, unknit.

The remaining interested parties were England, Denmark, Sweden-Norway, Holland and Russia, and they were required to place their bids in the presence of the Baltimore auctioneer, after all parties, including the United States, had been heard. The highest bidder would win possession of this polar ice-cap the market value of which was, to say the least, highly debatable.

Each of the five European states had its own private reasons for hoping to be the highest bidder.

Already in possession of the North Cape, above the 70th parallel, Sweden-Norway made no secret of her conviction that she had rights over the vast space that stretches as far as Spitsbergen and beyond, to the Pole itself. Indeed, the Norwegian Kheilhau and the celebrated Swede Nordenskiöld had contributed considerably to geographical advances in these regions.

Denmark argued as follows: that she was already sovereign of Iceland and the Faroe Islands, just about level with the Polar Circle; and that those colonies established in the Arctic regions also belonged to her, including Disko Island in the Davis Strait, the settlements of Holsteinborg, Proven, Godhavn and Upernavik in the Baffin Sea and along the western coast of Greenland. Moreover, the famous navigator Bering was of Danish extraction and, although he was serving Russia at the time, by 1728 he had crossed the strait to which he left his name, before going on to perish thirteen years later with thirty of his crew, on the coast of an island also now named after him. Previously, in 1619, the navigator Jean Munk had explored the eastern coast of Greenland and discovered several places previously unknown. Denmark, therefore, had a strong case to join the bidding.

As for Holland, it was her seamen Barentz and Heemskrek who had been visiting Spitsbergen and Novaya Zemlya since the end of the sixteenth century. It was one of its sons, Jan

Mayen, whose bold Northerly campaign had, in 1611, won his country possession of the eponymous island, located beyond the 71st degree of latitude. With such a past, Holland was bound to take part.

Moving on to the Russians, with Aleksei Chirikov who had Bering under his command; with Paulutsky, whose expedition of 1751 broached the borders of the Arctic Sea; with Captain Martin Spanberg and Lieutenant William Walton, who explored these unknown lands in 1739: they had played a valuable part in discoveries made around the strait that divides Asia and America. What is more, due to the position of the Siberian territories, extending for 120 degrees up to the far limits of Kamchatka, along the vast Asiatic coast, where Samoyeds, Yakuts, Chukchis and other peoples live under their authority, the Russians control a good half of the Northern Ocean. And then, at the 75th parallel, less than 900 miles from the pole, they also possess the islands and islets of New Siberia, that is, the Liatkov Archipelago, discovered at the beginning of the eighteenth century. In any case, in 1764, before the English, before the Americans, before the Swedish, the mariner Chichagov sought a north-east passage, in the hope of shortening the length of voyages between the two continents.

Nevertheless, it appeared that the Americans had a good case for becoming proprietors of this most inaccessible spot on the planet. They too had often tried to reach it, during the search for the missing Sir John Franklin, with Grinnel, Kane, Hayes, Greely, De Long and the other hardy explorers. They too could point to the geographic location of their country, which extends into the Polar Circle, from the Bering Strait as far as Hudson Bay. All these lands, all these islands: Wollaston, Prince Albert, Victoria, King William, Melville,

Cockburne, Banks, Baffin, not counting the thousand islets in that archipelago, were a kind of extension connecting America as far as the 90th degree. And then, if the North Pole *can* be seen as directly linked, almost without interruption, to one of the world's great continents, is it not rather to America than to protrusions of Asia or of Europe? Therefore, nothing could be more natural than that the proposal for acquisition be made by the federation on behalf of an American Society, and, to suppose that if any one power's rights over the Polar realm were beyond doubt, that Power could only be the United States of America.

All the same, it must be acknowledged that the United Kingdom, which also ruled Canada and British Columbia, whose many sailors had distinguished themselves in the Arctic campaigns, also presented substantial reasons for wishing to annex this part of the globe to her vast colonial empire. This set her newspapers arguing at length and passionately.

'Yes, without a doubt!' replied the great English geographer Kliptringan, in an article in *The Times* that made a great splash, 'Yes! The Swedes, Danes, Dutch, Russians and Americans may parade their rights. But England cannot, without losing face, allow this territory to slip through her fingers. Does the northern part of the new continent not already belong to us? These lands, these islands that make up the territory, were they not conquered by our own explorers, from Willoughby, who voyaged around Spitsbergen and Novaya Zemlya in 1739, up to Mac Clure, whose ship made it clear through the North-West Passage in 1853?'

'Besides,' declared the *Standard*, 'by the feather in Admiral Fizé's hat, were Frobisher, Davis, Hall, Weymouth, Hudson, Baffin, Cook, Ross, Parry, Bechey, Belcher, Franklin, Mulgrave, Scoresby, Mac Clintock, Kennedy, Nares, Collinson and Archer not Englishmen? Then what country could extend a better claim over that portion of the Arctic regions that its navigators have not yet reached?'

'That may be!' retorted the *San Diego Courier* (from California), 'We ought to assess this business on its own merits and, since there is the question of pride between the United States and United Kingdom, we could say: while the Englishman Markham, of the Nares expedition, has been as far as 83°20' of northern latitude, the Americans Lockwood and Brainard, of the Greely expedition, in outstripping him by fifteen minutes of a degree, have set the thirty-eight stars of the American flag twinkling at 83°35'. To them belongs the honour of having come the closest to the North Pole!'

Such were the attacks and such were the replies they received.

In any case, to usher in our series of explorers who have ventured into the midst of the Arctic regions, we ought also to cite the Venetian Cabot (1498) and the Portuguese Corte Real (1500) who discovered Greenland and Labrador. But neither Italy nor Portugal had thought of taking part in the auction, caring little about which state would be the winner.

As we might have predicted, it turned out that this battle would be contested with due vigour only by England and America, the pound fighting the dollar.

Nevertheless, those countries sharing borders with the Polar lands did discuss the offer formulated by the North Polar Exploitation Association in commercial and scientific meetings. Following much debate, they decided to join the bidding, which was to open on 3rd December in Baltimore, arming their respective delegates with strictly limited credit. As for the sum produced by the sale, this would be shared out between the five unsuccessful bidders, who would receive it in compensation, and renounce all future claims to the territory.

While there was no lack of discussion, all were agreed in the end. In addition, the interested parties accepted that the auction should take place in Baltimore, as the American government had suggested. Armed with their letters of credit, the delegates left London, The Hague, Stockholm, Copenhagen and St Petersburg, and arrived in the United States three weeks before the date fixed for the auction.

At this point, America still had no representative other than the man from the North Polar Exploitation Association, William S. Forster, whose name was the only one mentioned in the letter published in the *New York Herald* on 7th November.

But the European delegates were all chosen and named. They made a varied and interesting bunch.

For Holland: Jacques Jansen, former governor of the Dutch Indies, fifty-three years old, fat, short, barrel-chested, with small arms, little bowed legs, aluminium-framed spectacles, his face round and ruddy, a bush of hair, greying whiskers – a decent man, rather incredulous about this latest enterprise, the practical benefits of which quite escaped him.

For Denmark: Eric Baldenak, ex-deputy governor of the Danish territory in Greenland, of middling height, slightly uneven shoulders, pot-bellied, his head enormous and always on the move, so short-sighted that his nose touched his books and ledgers, unable to see reason in any matter concerning his country's rights, for he considered Denmark the legitimate ruler of all the Northern regions.

For Sweden-Norway: Jan Harald, a professor of cosmography in Christiania, who had been one of the keenest partisans of the Nordenskiöld expedition, a true man of the north, red-faced, his beard and hair a shade of blond reminiscent of overripe wheat – he was quite persuaded that, since it contained nothing apart from the Paleocrystic Sea, the polar icecap was quite valueless. Therefore, decidedly uninterested in the issue at hand, he was present only for the sake of good form.

For Russia: Colonel Boris Karkov, part military man, part diplomat, tall, stiff, with long hair, beard and moustache all of a piece, looking uncomfortable in his civvies and sub-consciously feeling for the handle of the sword he used to carry – he was very curious to know in particular what was behind the North Polar Exploitation Association's proposal and whether this might be the cause of future international disputes.

Finally, for England: Major Donellan and his secretary Dean Toodrink. These last two between them represented all the appetites, all the aspirations of the United Kingdom, her commercial and industrial instincts, her tendency to consider as belonging to her, as if by the law of nature, all northern, southern and equatorial territories as yet unclaimed by anyone else.

An Englishman if ever there was one, this Major Donellan was tall, thin, bony, nervous, angular, with the neck of a woodcock, head resembling Lord Palmerston on sloping shoulders, the legs of a marsh-wader, very spry for his sixty years, indefatigable – and this he had proved while working on the India/Burma border. He was never seen to laugh; perhaps he never had. Why ever should he? Have you ever seen a locomotive, or a crane or a steamer laugh?

In this, the major differed fundamentally from his secretary Dean Toodrink – a loquacious, pleasant youth, with a well-shaped head, locks of hair curling over his forehead and small screwed-up eyes. He was a Scot by birth, well known back in Auld Reekie for his light-hearted quips and his taste for practical jokes. Still, however cheerful he could be, he showed himself no less single-minded, determined and intransigent than Major Donellan when it came even to the least of Great Britain's claims.

These two delegates were clearly going to be the American Society's most obstinate adversaries. The North Pole was theirs: it had belonged to them since prehistoric times, as if the Creator had charged the English alone with ensuring the Earth's rotation on its axis, and they would be sure not to let the pole fall into the hands of foreigners.

It ought to be pointed out that, although France had not judged it necessary to send either an official or an unofficial delegate, a French engineer had come along for the love of it, hoping to follow this curious business very closely. We shall come to him in due course.

By now, the delegates of the northern powers of Europe had arrived in Baltimore, all by different ships, to avoid being influenced by each other. They were rivals. Each of them had in hand the necessary funding for the fight. But it is worth noting that they were not going in to battle with equal firepower. While one had at his disposal a sum well short of a million, another could call on a good deal more. And, really, for the purpose of acquiring a piece of our earth where it seemed man was destined never to set foot, even these sums might appear to some a good deal too much. In fact, the best endowed in this respect was the English delegate, to whom the United Kingdom had given access to a substantial sum of money. Thanks to this allowance, Major Donellan would not have much trouble beating his Swedish, Danish, Dutch and Russian adversaries. As for America, that was another story: it would be much tougher to beat her on dollars alone. Indeed, it was probable that the mysterious society would have considerable funds at its disposal. The war of wallets would be most vigorously contested by the United States and Great Britain.

With the arrival of the European delegates, the public imagination was gripped with renewed fervour. The oddest rumours circulated among the newspapers. Strange theories explaining this purchase of the North Pole began to appear. What could anyone really want with it? And what use could be made of it? None – unless it were to help maintain the icehouses of the Old and New Worlds. There was even one Parisian newspaper, the *Figaro*, that drolly offered this explanation. But this would still require some route to be cleared beyond the 84th parallel.

Having avoided each other during their transatlantic voyages, the delegates began to be a little more convivial once they had reached Baltimore, for the following reasons:

From the beginning, each of them had tried, individually and secretly, to make contact with the North Polar Exploitation Association. What they wanted to know, in order to benefit should the need arise, was the hidden motive behind this business and what profit the society hoped to make from it. Now, up to this point, nothing suggested that it had established an office in Baltimore. No office: no employees. 'For information, please apply to William S. Forster, the High Street.' Yet it did not seem that the honest cod-trader knew much more on the subject than the lowliest baggage-handler in town.

The delegates, then, could learn nothing from that quarter. They were reduced to considering the patently absurd conjectures circulating among the public. Would the society's secret remain a mystery for as long as her members chose not to divulge it? So the delegates feared. Certainly, the silence would not be broken until after the auction had been held.

It was natural that the delegates should end up meeting, should begin to call on each other, to sound each other out and finally to talk openly, perhaps – with hindsight – hoping to unite before their common enemy, that is, before the Americans.

So one day, on the evening of 22nd November, they were to be found in the midst of heated discussion at the Wolesley Hotel, in the apartment occupied by Major Donellan and his secretary Dean Toodrink. In fact, this move towards a common purpose was principally due to the skilful machinations of Colonel Boris Karkov, a superb diplomat.

At first, the conversation focused on the commercial and industrial advantages that the society might gain from the purchase of the Arctic. Professor Jan Harald asked whether any of his colleagues had been able to discover anything further on the subject. But, one by one, all admitted that they had tried to contact William S. Forster, to whom, according to the letter, communications should be addressed.

'But I got nowhere,' Eric Baldenak confessed.

'And I had no success,' added Jacques Jansen.

'As for me,' remarked Dean Toodrink, 'when I made enquiries among the shops on the High Street on behalf of Major Donellan, I found a stout gentleman dressed in black, with a top hat and wrapped in a white apron from his boots to his chin. When I asked him for information about the business, he replied that the *South Star* had just come in from Newfoundland with a full cargo, and he was all set to deliver a large batch of fresh cod on behalf of the house of Ardrinell & Co.'

'Aha!' countered the ever-sceptical former governor of the Dutch Indies, 'It's better business to buy a cargo of cod than to go throwing your money to the depths of a frozen sea!'

'That is entirely beside the point,' said Major Donellan then, in a curt and lofty tone. 'We're not talking about a shipment of cod but about the polar icecap…'

'Which America seems to want to clap on its own head!' finished Dean Toodrink, laughing at his own joke.

'It'll only catch cold,' Colonel Karkov trumped him.

'That is not the point,' the major said again, 'and I've no idea what this talk of headcolds is doing in the middle of our discussion. What's for sure is that, for one reason or another, America, as represented by the North Polar Exploitation Association – note the word "Exploitation", gentlemen – wishes to buy an area of 407,000 square miles over the North Pole, an area currently circumscribed – note the word "currently", gentlemen – by the 84th degree of latitude North…'

'That we know, Major Donellan,' retorted Jan Harald, 'only too well. But what we do not know is how the said society intends to use these lands, if they are lands, or these seas, if they are seas, from a commercial point of view…'

'That is not the point,' replied Major Donellan for a third time. 'A state intends to appropriate, by means of payment, a portion of the planet that, due to its geographical position, appears to belong more particularly to England…'

'To Russia,' said Colonel Karkov.

'To Holland,' said Jacques Jansen.

'To Sweden-Norway,' said Jan Harald.

'To Denmark,' said Eric Baldenak.

The five delegates' hackles had risen on cue and the meeting risked descending into vulgar squabbling, when Dean Toodrink ventured a contribution:

'Gentlemen,' he said in a conciliatory tone, 'this is not the point, to borrow the formulation of which my superior, Major Donellan, makes such liberal use. Since it is to all intents and purposes agreed that the circumpolar regions shall be put up for auction, they shall necessarily become the possession of whichever of the states you represent puts in the highest bid. Therefore, since Sweden-Norway, Russia, Denmark, Holland and England have put certain funds at their delegates' disposal, would it not be best to form a cooperative association, which would allow such a large sum to be bid that the American Society could never outbid them?'

The delegates looked at each other. This Dean Toodrink might just have found the answer. A cooperative… Nowadays, this word is the answer to everything. Just as we breathe, drink, eat and sleep, so too do we cooperate. Nothing could be more modern – whether in business or politics.

All the same, some opposition, or at least an explanation, was required, and Jacques Jansen spoke for his fellow delegates when he said:

'And then what? …'

'Yes indeed! … After the cooperative acquisition had been made?'

'But it seems to me that England…!' replied the Major stiffly.

'And Russia…!' said the Colonel, whose brows were darkly knit.

'And Holland…!' said the governor.

'When God gave Denmark to the Danish…' remarked Eric Baldenak.

'Excuse me,' Toodrink interrupted, 'but there is only one God-given country – and that is Scotland, to the Scots!'

'And why is that?' responded the Swedish delegate.

'Did the poet not say: Deus nobis *Ecotia* fecit?' retorted our wag, providing his own translation of the *hoec otia* from the sixth line of Virgil's first eclogue.

Everyone laughed – apart from Major Donellan – and for a second time the discussion was diverted from the unfortunate turn it was taking.

At this point, Dean Toodrink was able to add: 'Let us not quarrel, gentlemen! What good can that do?... Let us rather form our cooperative...'

'And then what?' said Jan Harald once more.

'Then?' replied Toodrink. 'Nothing could be simpler, gentlemen. Once you have bought it, the polar region shall either remain your joint property or, in return for reasonable compensation, you shall make it over to one of your co-purchasers. But your main goal will then have been achieved, that is, the definitive elimination of American participation!'

There was some sense to this proposition, at least for now, given that in the near future, these same delegates would be at each other's throats when it came to deciding the ultimate purchaser of this property that was as troublesome as it was useless. In any case, as Dean Toodrink had so cleverly demonstrated, the United States would by then be entirely out of the running.

'A sensible plan, in my view,' said Eric Baldenak.

'Nifty,' said Colonel Karkov.

'Adroit,' said Jan Harald.

'Cunning,' said Jacques Jansen.

'Thoroughly English!' approved Major Donellan.

Each had said his piece, in the hope of duping his worthy colleagues later on.

'So, gentlemen,' resumed Boris Karkov, 'is it quite agreed that, if we do form a cooperative, each state's rights shall be reserved for the future?'

It was agreed.

It remained only for the delegates to reveal the different sums that each state had put at their disposal. The amounts would be added together, and it was probable that the total would make such a significant sum that the North Polar Exploitation Association's resources would quite outstripped.

The question was raised by Dean Toodrink.

But this was quite another story. Total silence. Nobody felt like replying. Show their purses? Empty their pockets into the cooperative's coffers? Reveal in advance exactly how high each was hoping to bid? ... There was no need to rush into anything. What if some disagreement occurred later between the new cooperative's members? And what if changing circumstances obliged them to strike out for themselves? What if Karkov, the diplomat, drew the line at Jacques Jansen's game-playing, who took offence at Eric Baldenak's underhand machinations, who was irritated by Jan Harald's wiles, who then refused to back Major Donellan's lofty claims, who, in his turn, would hardly hesitate to plot against every one of his colleagues? In short, declaring one's financial resources meant showing one's hand just when it was crucial to play it close to one's chest.

Truly, there were only two ways to respond to Dean Toodrink's fair but indiscreet request. Either to exaggerate one's funds – which would have become highly embarrassing when it came to making payments – or to underplay them to such an extent that the whole exercise would degenerate into a joke and nothing more would come of the proposition.

The latter idea occurred first to the ex-governor of the Dutch Indies, who, we must admit, was not a serious man, and all his colleagues followed his lead.

'Sirs,' Holland pronounced through its spokesman, 'I am sorry to say it, but, for the purpose of acquiring the Arctic territory, all I have at my disposal is fifty rixdalers.'

'And I, no more than thirty-five roubles,' said Russia.

'And I, just twenty kronor,' said Sweden-Norway.

'And I, only fifteen krones,' said Denmark.

'Well,' Major Donellan said, in a voice that expressed every inch of the disdain that comes so naturally to Great Britons, 'it shall be for your benefit that we make this purchase, gentlemen, for England can contribute no more than one shilling and sixpence!'*

And, with that withering declaration, the conference of delegates from Old Europe came to an end.

* 1 rixdaler = 5.21 francs; one rouble = 3.92 francs; one kronor = 1.32 francs; one krone = 1.32 francs; one shilling = 1.15 francs

III

IN WHICH THE ARCTIC
IS PUT UP FOR AUCTION

Strangely, this sale of 3rd December was allocated an ordinary auction room where, usually, only house fittings and furnishings, tools and kitchen utensils, gadgets, etc, or artworks, paintings, statues, medals and antiques were sold. Given that the sale concerned land, shouldn't it take place either in the presence of a notary or before a court specially appointed for this type of procedure? And why was an auctioneer involved, when the item up for sale was in fact a section of our planet? Why should this slice of the sphere be treated just like a piece of furniture, despite being, above all, the most immovable thing in the world?

It all seemed quite illogical. And yet, that was the plan. The whole of the Arctic would be sold under these conditions, and the sale would be no less legitimate for it. This might be seen as suggesting that, in the view of the North Polar Exploitation Association, the land in question had something provisional about it, as if, in fact, it were possible to shift it. Indeed, this peculiarity began to intrigue a few eminently perspicacious minds – very rare, even in the United States.

There was actually a precedent. A portion of the planet had already gone under the hammer of an auctioneer at a public sale. And that was in America, to boot.

A few years previously, at San Francisco, an island in the Pacific, Spencer Island*, had been sold to the wealthy William W. Kolderup, who beat his nearest rival, J.R. Taskinar

* See *School for Crusoes* (*L'Ecole des Robinsons*) by the same author.

of Stockton, to the prize by $500,000. This Spencer Island had gone for four million dollars. It was, it is true, a habitable island, only a few degrees off the California coast, with forests, waterways, substantial and fertile ground, fields and prairies suitable for cultivation – not, like the North Pole, a vague area that might even be an ocean, covered with unmeltable ice and barred by impenetrable ice fields, very probably uninhabitable by anyone, ever. It was therefore reasonable to suppose that, when put to auction, the ill-defined polar realm would not fetch anything approaching such a price.

Nevertheless, on the day, the oddness of the business meant that serious experts were outnumbered by a large number of curious onlookers, all avid to witness the outcome. All in all, the battle promised to be an interesting one.

Moreover, since their arrival in Baltimore, the European delegates had been mobbed: they were much sought-after and, of course, much interviewed. As the event was taking place in America, public opinion was keyed up to the highest degree, which led to a betting craze – the most usual form by which over-excitement is manifest in the United States, although Europe now widely follows her lead in this habit. While US citizens – those of New England as much as those from central, western and southern states – divided into groups with opposing views, all were naturally rooting for their country. They were indeed hoping that the North Pole would take its place on the banner with the other thirty-eight stars. And yet, they were not without a degree of anxiety. It was not Russia, nor Sweden-Norway, nor Denmark, nor Holland, whose chances, which were negligible, were worrying them. But the United Kingdom was there with all her territorial ambition, her tendency to absorb everything, her well-known tenacity and her all-conquering banknotes. In view of this, large sums were called into play. Bets were laid on *America* and on *Great Britain* as if they were race-horses, until the betting factions, at least, were neck and neck. As for *Denmark*, *Sweden*, *Holland* and *Russia*, although they were touted with odds of 12–1 and 13.5–1, there were scarcely any takers.

The sale was scheduled for midday. All morning, a crowd of curious onlookers had been holding up the traffic in Bolton Street. Speculation had been running high since the day before. The papers had just learnt, by transatlantic cable, that the majority of bets, placed by Americans, were held by the English, and Dean Toodrink had immediately posted the odds up in the auction room. It was rumoured that the government of Great Britain had put considerable funds in Major Donellan's hands… The lords of the Admiralty, the *New York Herald* observed, were pushing to acquire the Arctic territories, earmarked in advance for inclusion in the catalogue of English colonies.

What truth was there in this news, what likelihood in this gossip? No one knew. But, that day in Baltimore, the thinking among sober people was that if the North Polar Exploitation Association were left to its own resources, the battle might well end in England's favour. Hence the pressure that the most enthusiastic Americans sought to apply to their government in Washington. In the midst of this excitement, the brand new society, as represented in the modest person of its agent William S. Forster, appeared unperturbed by the general fuss, as if it had no doubt about its success.

As the hour approached, the crowds massed along Bolton Street. Three hours before the doors were due to open, it was no longer possible to reach the auction room. Already the whole area reserved for members of the public was filled to bursting. Only a few seats, marked off by a barrier, had been kept for the European delegates, so they could follow the progress of the auction and make their bids in good time.

Eric Baldenak, Boris Karkof, Jacques Jansen, Jan Harald, Major Donellan and his secretary Dean Toodrink were seated there. They made a compact, close-knit group, like soldiers in attack formation. You could almost imagine they were about to launch an attack on the North Pole.

On the American side, nobody had come forward apart from the cod contractor, whose vulgar face expressed the most perfect indifference. He appeared the least perturbed by his vast audience and was no doubt thinking about storage for the cargoes he was expecting from the ships bound for Newfoundland. So who were the capitalists represented by this good man, who might be about to pour forth millions of dollars? The question sparked even greater excitement in this curious audience.

Indeed, no one would have suspected that J-T Maston and Mrs Evangelina Scorbitt had anything to do with the business. How could anyone know? Both were present, however, though invisible in the crowd, not having special seats, surrounded by some of the principal members of the Baltimore Gun Club, who were also Maston's colleagues. They appeared to be entirely disinterested spectators of the proceedings. William S. Forster himself seemed not to recognize them.

Contrary to the regular practice of auction houses, it wasn't possible to organize a public viewing of the object that was up for sale. The North Pole could not be passed from hand to hand, nor inspected from every angle, nor examined by magnifying glass, nor rubbed with a finger to see if the patina were real or artificial, as one would for any other antique. And yet, antique it was – predating the Iron, Bronze and Stone Ages, in fact all the prehistoric epochs, since it was there when the world began.

Still, while the pole could not be there on the auctioneer's desk, a large map, in full view of the interested parties, showed the configuration of the Arctic regions by means of coloured sections. At 17° above the Polar Circle, a very distinct red line, following the 84th parallel, circumscribed the part of the world whose sale the North Polar Exploitation Association had provoked. It certainly appeared that the region was entirely taken up by a sea, covered with a frozen carapace of considerable thickness. But that was the buyer's concern. They would not, at least, be misled as to the nature of the goods.

On the stroke of noon, Andrew R. Gilmour, the auctioneer, came in by a small door set in the wood panels of the room's far side and took his place in front of his desk. Already Flint, the stentorian bid-caller, was pacing heavily, with the swaying gait of a caged bear, along the length of the barrier that held back the public. Both were savouring the thought that this auction would send a very substantial percentage their way which they would take great pleasure in pocketing. Naturally this would be a cash purchase. As for the sum itself, however large, the whole of this would go to the delegates representing those states whose bids had been unsuccessful.

At that moment, the auction house clock's jangling bell announced to those outside – call it *urbi et orbi* – that the bidding was about to begin.

It was a solemn moment. All hearts beat fast in the neighbourhood and throughout the town. From Bolton Street and its adjacent streets, an insistent murmur, fed and spread by the milling crowds, reached the ears of those inside the auction room.

Andrew R. Gilmour was obliged to wait until the deafening tumult of rabble and babble had subsided before he could begin to speak.

Then, he stood up and looked round at his audience. Allowing his pince-nez to drop back onto his chest, he said with a hint of emotion:

'Gentlemen, upon the proposition of the federal government and according to the agreement afforded this proposition by the various states of the New World and also of the Old Continent, we are able to put up for sale a lot made up of real estate situated around the North Pole, to the extent of and including everything within the current bounds of the 84th parallel, in the form of continents, seas, straits, islands, islets, ice floes; that is: all solid and liquid aspects whatsoever.'

Then, pointing a finger at the wall:

'Be so good as to glance at the map, which has been drawn in accordance with the most recent discoveries. You will see that the surface of this lot consists very approximately of a stretch of 407,000 uninterrupted square miles. Therefore, for the sake of practicality, it has been decided that bids should be made per square mile. A bid of one cent will therefore be equivalent, in round figures, to 407,000 cents; and one dollar, 407,000 dollars. – Quiet please, gentlemen!'

The request was necessary, because the crowd's impatience manifested itself in a tumult over which the voices of bidders would struggle to be heard.

As soon as a modicum of silence had been established, thanks principally to the intervention of the caller Flint, who bellowed like a ship's foghorn in the mist, Andrew R. Gilmour continued with these words:

'Before we open the bidding, I must remind you again of one of this auction's conditions: no matter what geographical or meteorological modifications may affect it in the future, the polar estate, as circumscribed by the 84th degree of latitude

North, shall belong indisputably to the highest bidder and its ownership cannot be contested by the other bidders.'

Once again, that phrase about 'geographical or meteorological modifications' provoked amusement in some but made others rather thoughtful.

'I declare the auction open!' said the auctioneer in ringing tones.

And, with his ivory hammer trembling in his hand, in the jargon endemic to his line of work, he added in a nasal voice:

'We have a taker here at ten cents a square mile!'

At ten cents, or a tenth of a dollar, that came to a total of $40,700 for the entirety of the Arctic property.

Whether or not the auctioneer Andrew R. Gilmour really had a taker at that price, the bid was straightaway bettered by Eric Baldenak on behalf of the Danish government.

'Twenty cents!' he offered.

'Thirty cents!' said Jacques Jansen, 'for Holland.'

'Thirty-five,' said Jan Harald, 'for Sweden-Norway.'

'Forty,' countered Boris Karkov, 'on behalf of all the Russias.'

Already this represented a sum of $162, 800, though the bidding had only just begun.

It was noted that Great Britain's representative had so far neither opened his mouth nor even unsealed his lips, which were tightly pursed.

For his part, the cod contractor William S. Forster remained in stony silence. He appeared to be absorbed in reading the *Newfoundland Mercurial*, which lists consignments and daily rates for the American markets.

'Forty cents, I have forty cents per square mile,' repeated Flint, rounding off his statement in a kind of trilling flourish, 'going for forty cents!'

Major Donellan's four colleagues stared at each other. Had they, then, been outbid at the very start of the struggle? Were they already reduced to silent spectators?

'Come now, gentlemen,' Andrew R. Gilmour went on, 'raise me forty cents! Who'll go higher? Forty cents! It's worth a bit more than that, the polar ice-cap...'

You might have expected him to add:

'...guaranteed 100 per cent pure ice.'

But the Danish delegate had just spoken:

'Fifty cents!'

And the Dutch delegate too, outbidding him by ten cents.

'Sixty cents per square mile!' cried Flint. 'Sixty cents, going... Won't anyone raise me?'

Those 'sixty cents' already came to the very respectable sum of \$244,200.*

Now the watching crowd greeted the Dutch bid with a murmur of satisfaction. It was a strange and very human thing: the shabby, penniless wretches who filled the room, the poor devils without a dime to rub between them, appeared to be the most excited by this battle conducted in dollar-bill blows.

Nevertheless, after Jacques Jansen's interjection, Major Donellan looked up and then towards his secretary Dean Toodrink. However, upon a barely perceptible negative sign from the latter, he remained silent.

As for William S. Forster, still deeply immersed in the perusal of his market rates, he was pencilling a few marginal notes.

And as for J-T Maston, he was nodding mildly in response to Mrs Evangelina Scorbitt's smiles.

* 1,221,000 francs

'Come now, gentlemen, show a little spirit! We are lagging here! Very slow indeed! Where's your fire?' added Andrew R Gilmour. 'Well I never – no more bids? We shall have to knock it down…'

And his hammer was rising and falling like a holy water sprinkler in the hands of the parish verger.

'Seventy cents!' added Professor Jan Harald, unable to conceal the slight shake in his voice.

'Eighty!' retorted Colonel Boris Karkov almost instantly.

'There we go!… Eighty cents!' cried Flint, whose great round eyes fired up as the bidding took off once more.

A wink from Dean Toodrink had the Major jumping up like a jack-in-the-box.

'One hundred cents!' said Great Britain's representative, brusquely.

These words alone committed England to $407, 000.

Those betting on the United Kingdom gave a great cheer, which was echoed among some of the other spectators.

Those betting on America looked at each other in some disappointment. Four hundred and seven thousand dollars? That was already a substantial amount to pay for this whimsy of a North Polar estate. Four hundred and seven thousand dollars' worth of icebergs, ice fields and ice floes!

What about the man from the North Polar Exploitation Association, who did not breathe a word, who did not even look up? Would he never get round to placing a bid? If he meant to wait until the Danish, Swedish, Dutch and Russian delegates had run out of funds, it appeared that that moment had arrived. Indeed, their expressions suggested that Major Donellan's 'One hundred cents' was their signal to abandon the battlefield.

'I have one hundred cents a square mile!' resumed the auctioneer.

'One hundred cents!... A hundred cents! A hundred cents!' repeated his caller Flint, using his half-closed fist as a loudspeaker.

'Won't anyone raise me!' Andrew R. Gilmour took up again. 'Are we closed? Done and dusted? No regrets? Is it time for the hammer...?'

And he tightened the grip of his hammer hand, while glaring provocatively around at the assembled crowd, whose muttering petered out into a tense silence.

'Once? ... Twice? ...' he went on.

'One hundred and twenty cents,' said William R. Forster, calmly, not even glancing up, after turning a page of his newspaper.

'Hooray!' cried those bettors who made the biggest bets on the United States of America.

Major Donellan rose again, in his turn. His long neck swivelled mechanically on the base formed by his shoulders and his lips jutted outwards like a beak. He glared at the American company's impassive representative, but was unable to induce any reaction – even as they eyeballed each other. That devil William S. Forster would not budge.

'A hundred and forty,' said Major Donellan.

'Hundred and sixty,' Forster shot back.

'A hundred and eighty,' called out the major.

'Hunner n' ninety,' muttered Forster.

'One hundred and ninety-five cents!' roared the British delegate.

At this, crossing his arms, he appeared to lay down a challenge to all thirty-eight states of the Federation.

You could have heard an ant go for a stroll, a trout swim upstream, a butterfly flutter, a larva crawl, a microbe change direction. Every heart was thumping. Everyone's life depended on Major Donellan's mouth. His head, usually so mobile, no longer moved an inch. As for Dean Toodrink, he was scratching the back of his head so fiercely as almost to draw blood.

Andrew R. Gilmour allowed a few seconds to pass, each of which felt like a century. The cod trader went on reading his paper and noting down figures that evidently had nothing to do with the business at hand. Was it that he, too, had come to the end of his resources? Would he relinquish his chance to make a last bid? Was it that this sum of 195 cents per square mile, or more than $793,000 for the whole property, seemed, to him too, to have reached the outer limits of absurdity?

'One hundred and ninety-five cents!' said the auctioneer, again. 'We shall proceed to knock down…'

And his hammer was on the point of falling back to the table.

'One hundred and ninety-five cents!' repeated the bid-caller. 'Take it!… It's a sale!…'

This plea rose up from several impatient spectators, as if to rebuke Andrew R. Gilmour for his hesitation.

'Once… twice…!' he called.

And all eyes were trained on the North Polar Exploitation Association's man.

And he? This surprising person was in the process of blowing his nose, lengthily, into a large checked handkerchief, and thus severely compressing his nasal passages.

Still, J-T Maston's eyes bored into him, while Mrs Evangelina Scorbitt's were trained in the same direction. The violence of the emotion they were trying to master was visible from their pallor. Why was William S. Forster hesitating to outbid Major Donellan?

William S. Forster blew his nose a second time, and then a third, with the noise of a veritable fusillade of fireworks. Yet, between the last two honks, he had proffered in a tone of gentle humility:

'Two hundred cents!'

A long shudder passed through the room. Then the Americans' cheers rang out loud enough to set the windows rattling.

Overwhelmed, crushed, flattened, Major Donellan dropped back into his seat beside Dean Toodrink, who was no less crestfallen than he. At this price per square mile, the total would come to a huge $814,000, and it was immediately plain that the British purse could stretch no further.

'Two hundred cents!' repeated Andrew R Gilmour.

'Two hundred cents!' trumpeted Flint.

'Going once… going twice!' the auctioneer went on. 'Will no one raise me?'

Prompted by a seemingly involuntary impulse, Major Donellan stood up once more and looked around at the other delegates. He represented their one remaining hope of stopping the North Polar lands from slipping through European fingers. But his effort was to be Europe's last. The major opened his mouth, closed it again, and England – in the form of this fine officer – sank back onto the bench.

'Gone!' called out Andrew Gilmour, striking the table with the head of his ivory hammer.

'Three cheers for the United States!' chanted the triumphant victors of America.

In an instant, the news of the acquisition spread through the neighbourhoods of Baltimore; then, by aerial connections, over the length and breadth of the whole Federation; then, by submarine wires, it was rushed to the Old World.

So it was that the North Polar Exploitation Association, through the offices of its straw man, William S. Forster, became proprietor of the Arctic realm, of all that lay within the 84th parallel.

And the following day, when William S. Forster went to reveal who was behind the bid, the name he gave was that of Impey Barbicane, whose company was Barbicane & Co.

IV

IN WHICH OLD ACQUAINTANCES RESURFACE

'Barbicane & Co'. The president of a gun club. What could gun-lovers possibly have to do with an operation of this kind? We shall see.

It may – or may not – be necessary to provide a formal introduction to Impey Barbicane of Baltimore, the Gun Club President, and Captain Nicholl and J-T Maston and Tom Hunter with his wooden legs and the dashing Bilsby and Colonel Bloomsberry, and all their other colleagues. These odd characters may be some twenty years older since the last time the world's eyes were trained on them, but they have not really changed: just as corporeally incomplete, yet just as loud, as audacious, as devil-may-care, when it comes to dashing head-first into another extraordinary adventure. Time has made little difference to this bevy of retired gun-men. It has respected them, as it respects the decommissioned cannons that furnish the museums of former arsenals.

If the Gun Club counted 1,833 members at the time of its foundation – we are talking about persons here, not about members in the sense of arms and legs, the majority of the former being already rather short of the latter – and if 30,575 correspondents used to pride themselves on their connection with the club, these figures had in no way diminished in the intervening years. On the contrary. Indeed, thanks to the unlikely attempt it had made to establish a direct means of

* See, by the same author, *De la Terre à la Lune* ('From the Earth to the Moon') and *Autour de la Lune* ('Around the Moon')

communication between the Earth and the Moon,* the club's fame had grown by a huge proportion.

No one had forgotten the sensation caused by this memorable experiment, which is worth summarizing in a few lines.

Some years after America's Civil War, bored by the absence of further excitement, a few members of the Gun Club had come up with a plan to send a projectile to the Moon using a monstrous cannon known as a Columbiad. One of these cannon, 900 feet long, with a 9 feet diameter bore, had been cast in Moon City, on the Florida Peninsula, and charged with 400,000 pounds of gun cotton. Fired by this cannon, an aluminium cylindro-conical shell had flown towards the Queen of the Night using the force generated by 6 billion litres of petrol. Having flown right around the moon, as a result of a deviation in its trajectory, the shell had fallen back to Earth, where it was swallowed up by the Pacific at latitude 27°7' North and longitude 41°37' West. It was in these waters that the frigate *Susquehanna*, of the federal fleet, had fished it up to the ocean's surface, to the great relief of its passengers.

And indeed, there were passengers. Two of the Gun Club's members, its president Impey Barbicane and Captain Nicholl, accompanied by a Frenchman who was well-known for his feats of fearless intrepidity, had taken passage inside this projectile-carriage. All three had returned from their journey safe and sound. However, while the two Americans were still members of the club, quite ready to risk some brand-new adventure, the Frenchman, Michel Ardan, was no longer with them. On returning to Europe, it appeared he had made his fortune – to the surprise of many – and was right now not only showing off his cake, but also eating it and even licking the spoon, if we are to believe the most reliable reports.

After this bombshell, Impey Barbicane and Nicholl had enjoyed their celebrity in relative peace. But still thirsting for great projects, they dreamt of the next enterprise of this kind. They were not lacking in money. Some funds remained from their last exploit – almost $200,000 out of the $5.5 million that had been raised for them by public subscription in both New and Old Worlds. In addition, simply by travelling all over the United States and exhibiting themselves inside their aluminium projectile, like circus attractions in a cage, they had gathered further rich takings and basked in all the glory that the most ambitious human achievements may confer.

Impey Barbicane and Captain Nicholl might have been content with this, were they not eaten up with boredom. It was to raise themselves out of their torpor that they had just bought the Arctic.

However, we must not forget that this purchase was only possible at a price of more than $800,000 because Mrs Evangelina Scorbitt had contributed the necessary additional funds. Thanks to this generous lady, Europe was beaten by America.

Her generosity can be explained as follows:

Since their return, while President Barbicane and Captain Nicholl had been enjoying unrivalled celebrity, someone else was also attracting his share of attention. It was J-T Maston, the Gun Club's fiery secretary. This skilled calculator was responsible for the formulae that had made the great lunar experiment possible. It was not fear that prevented him joining his two colleagues on their extra-terrestrial voyage, not at all. But the worthy gunner, lacking a right hand, had also been fitted with a skull made of rubber, following one of those accidents that are all too common in war. Showing him to the Moon-dwellers would have given them a poor impression of the Earth's inhabitants, for whom the Moon is, after all, no more than a humble satellite.

To his deep regret, J-T Maston had had to resign himself to staying behind. Nevertheless, he had not been idle. After overseeing the construction of an immense telescope and its installation on the summit of Long's Peak, one of the tallest of the Rocky Mountains, he had made his way there, so that, from the moment the projectile came into view, describing its majestic arc across the sky, he could remain at the observation post night and day. There, at the eyepiece of the gigantic instrument, he had done his best to keep track of his friends, as their aerial vehicle zoomed out into space.

It seemed as if they were forever lost to the Earth, those audacious voyagers, once they had been lured by lunar gravity into a new orbit, which it was assumed had compelled the projectile to revolve eternally around the night star like a satellite of the moon itself. But the assumption was wrong. A deflection, that you might call heaven-sent, modified the projectile's direction. Having gone around the Moon instead of landing on it, and then been drawn into a progressively accelerating fall, the projectile had flown back to our planet, travelling at a speed equal to 170,000 miles per hour at the moment when it was sucked down to the depths of the sea.

Luckily, the liquid mass of the Pacific had cushioned the plunge, which was witnessed by the American frigate *Susquehanna*. The news was straight away transmitted to J-T Maston. The Gun Club's secretary returned in haste from the observatory at Long's Peak, in order to direct the rescue. Soundings were made in the area where the projectile had crashed and the devoted J-T Maston was prepared to don a deep-sea diver's outfit in order to retrieve his friends.

In fact, such lengths turned out to be unnecessary. Displacing a quantity of water superior to its actual weight, after accomplishing a superb dive, the aluminium projectile had floated back up to the surface of the Pacific. It was in these conditions that President Barbicane, Captain Nicholl and Michel Ardan were found on the ocean's surface: they were playing dominoes inside their floating prison.

Now, J-T Maston's role in these extraordinary adventures had brought him squarely into the public eye.

Certainly, he was not a handsome man, with his artificial cranium and his right forearm fixed up with a metal hook. Nor was he young, either, having fifty-eight good years behind him at the time this account begins. But the originality of his character, the liveliness of his intelligence, the fire that lit his gaze, the passion he brought to everything he did, had made him a kind of ideal man in Mrs Evangelina Scorbitt's eyes. In any case, his brain was intact, carefully stored beneath its rubber skullcap, and he continued to pass – and rightly – for one of the most remarkable calculators of his time.

Now, even though the most minor sums gave her a migraine, Mrs Evangelina Scorbitt had a taste for mathematicians. She considered them creatures from a separate – and superior – species. Heads in which Xs bounce about like walnuts in a sack, brains for which algebraic signs are mere child's play, hands that juggle triple integrals like a tightrope-walker with his glasses and bottles, minds that find meaning in formulae such as the following: $\iiint \rho(x\ y\ z)\ dx\ dy\ dz$ – these wise minds seemed to her to merit every admiration and be perfectly formed to attract a woman in proportion to their mass and in inverse ratio to the square of their distance. Indeed, J-T Maston was quite corpulent enough to exercise an irresistible attraction on her, and as for distance, she would make sure that was absolutely nil, were they ever to find themselves alone together.

This, it has to be said, did rather trouble the Gun Club's secretary, who had never sought happiness in such close associations. Besides, Mrs Evangelina Scorbitt was no longer in the first flush of youth – nor even the second – with her forty-five years, her hair plastered to her temples like a piece of much-dyed worsted, her mouth rather too full of over-long teeth of which she had not shed a single one, her un-contoured waist, her graceless gait. In short, she appeared like an old maid, even though she had been married – only for a few years, it is true. But she was an excellent person, whose paradise on earth would be complete were she only allowed to be introduced in the Baltimore salons by the name of Mrs J-T Maston.

The widow's fortune was very substantial. She was not as rich as the Goulds, the Mackays, the Vanderbilts or the Gordon Bennetts, whose fortunes ran into the billions and who could have offered charity to a Rothschild. She wasn't in possession of $300 million, as was Mrs Moses Carper, $200 million, like Mrs Stewart, or $80 million like Mrs Crocker – and widows all three, let's not forget! – nor was she rich on the scale of Mrs Hammersley, Mrs Helly Green, Mrs Maffitt, Mrs Marshall, Mrs Para Stevens, Mrs Mintury and several others. Nevertheless, there was a seat kept for her at that memorable banquet at the Fifth Avenue Hotel in New York, to which the only guests admitted are five times millionaires. In fact, Mrs Evangelina Scorbitt's resources amounted to a good three million dollars, her legacy from John P. Scorbitt, whose fortune had been made by trading in the parallel worlds of fashion articles and salted pork. In any case, the generous widow would have been delighted to spend her entire fortune on J-T Maston, on whom she could also bestow a bottomless trove of tenderness.

In the meantime, upon J-T Maston's request, Mrs Evangelina Scorbitt had willingly agreed to put a few hundred thousand dollars into the North Polar Exploitation Association's project, without even knowing what it was. It is true that J-T Maston's involvement guaranteed the project would be no less than grandiose, sublime, superhuman. The Gun Club secretary's past would vouch for his future.

It seems very likely that, after the auction, once she had learned that the new Society's governing board would be led by the President of the Gun Club, under the corporate name of Barbicane & Co, she was filled with confidence. And since J-T Maston was part of the 'and Co.', she could congratulate herself on becoming its leading shareholder.

Thus Mrs Evangelina Scorbitt found herself majority proprietor of that portion of the northern regions circumscribed by the 84th parallel. All to the good. But what would she do with it, or rather, how did the Society intend her to profit in any way from this inaccessible realm?

The question remained, and while, from the point of view of her pecuniary interests, it was of serious interest to Mrs Evangelina Scorbitt, it was also fascinating to the rest of the world, out of common curiosity.

This excellent lady had indeed – very discreetly, of course – tried to broach the subject with J-T Maston, before putting her capital at the disposal of the project's promoters. But J-T Maston had invariably responded with the greatest reticence. Mrs Evangelina Scorbitt would soon find out what was afoot, but not before the time came to dazzle the world by informing it of the brand-new society's plans.

Doubtless he was thinking of this as an enterprise that, as Rousseau put it, 'was unprecedented and would be inimitable'*, a project destined to far outstrip the Gun Club members' attempt to enter into direct communication with the moon.

However she protested, J-T Maston would only lay his finger on her parted lips and say: 'Dear Mrs Scorbitt, have faith!'

And, if Mrs Evangelina Scorbitt had had faith 'before', what immense joy would she feel 'afterwards', when the hot-headed secretary held her responsible for the United States of America's triumph and the defeat of all northern Europe!

'But may I not at last know now...?' she asked, smiling at the eminent calculator.

'You shall know soon!' replied J-T Maston, shaking the hand of his co-partner vigorously – in the American style.

This handshake had the immediate effect of calming Mrs Evangelina Scorbitt's impatience.

A few days later, the Old and New Worlds were no less shaken – not to mention the shaking awaiting them by and by – on learning of the patently crazy project for the purpose of which the North Polar Exploitation Association was about to resort to a public subscription.

It turned out that the society had acquired this portion of the circumpolar regions for the sole purpose of developing... the North Polar coalmines!

* [See the *Confessions*: 'n'eut jamais d'exemple et qui n'aura point d'imitateurs'.]

V

BUT FIRST, IS THERE REALLY
COAL AT THE NORTH POLE?

This was the first question to occur to the minds of those with a logical frame of mind.

'Why should there be coal seams around the Pole?' asked some.

'Why should there not be?' responded others.

As we know, layers of coal, which are distributed through many parts of the planet's surface, abound in many European countries. As for the two Americas, they possess considerable such resources, of which perhaps the United States is the more plentifully provided. Similar layers are also present in Africa, Asia and Oceania.

As our knowledge of the planet's various landmasses advances, so we are discovering these layers at every geological level, as anthracite in the oldest sites, as coal in higher, carboniferous strata, as stipite in secondary strata and as lignite in tertiary strata. This mineral fuel will not run out for a period which can be counted in the hundreds of years.

Yet, around the world, the extraction of coal, of which England alone produces 60 million tonnes, has reached an annual rate of 400 million tonnes. Now, this rate of consumption shows every sign of increasing while our industrial needs likewise continue to grow. Even if electricity replaces steam as a source of power, it will entail the same rate of coal consumption for the production of that power. The belly of industry hungers for coal alone; it consumes nothing else. Industry is a 'carboniverous' animal; there is no choice but to feed it.

Besides, this coal is not only our fuel, it also forms the very substance of this Earth, from which science currently makes the majority of its products and by-products. Thanks to the transformations it undergoes in scientific crucibles, we are able to dye, to sweeten, to flavour, to spray, to purify, to heat, to illuminate, even to ornament, due to our production of diamonds from it. Coal is as useful as iron; more useful, even.

Luckily, we shall never run out of the latter metal; it is the very foundation of our planet.

Really, the Earth should be thought of as a more or less carbonate mass of iron in its fluid igneous state, covered with liquid silicates, a kind of slag over which are laid our solid rocks and water. The other metals, as well as the water and rock, make up only the tiniest fraction of our planet's composition.

But, while our iron consumption is provided for to the end of days, our appetite for coal is not. Far from it. Wise people with an eye on the future, even when that future may be hundreds of years away, ought to seek out coalmines wherever far-sighted nature left them in the geological eras.

'Perfect!' replied the nay-sayers sarcastically.

For, in the United States as elsewhere, people are to be found who, through envy or odium, prefer to disparage others, and others who contradict for the pure pleasure of contradiction.

'Perfect!' said the nay-sayers. 'But, why should there be coal at the North Pole?'

'Why?' echoed President Barbicane's supporters. 'Because, in all likelihood, at the time these geological formations were laid down, the Sun's volume was such that, according to Monsieur Blandet's theory, the difference in temperature between the equator and the poles was scarcely measurable.

At that time, immense forests covered the northern areas of the planet, well before men appeared, at which point our planet was subject to the sustained effects of heat and humidity.'

This is what the newspapers, magazines and reviews that were committed supporters of the society were confirming in a thousand different articles, some humorous, some scientific. These forests, being sunk in swamps during the vast convulsions that shook the Earth before she achieved her final, definitive form, had unquestionably been transformed into coal, due to the action of time, water and the Earth's internal heat. So, nothing could be more probable than this hypothesis that the polar regions are rich in coal deposits, only waiting to be revealed under the miner's pick.

Besides, there were facts – undeniable facts. Even those people who hate relying on mere probabilities judged them watertight; they were even sufficient to justify research into the different kinds of coal present at the surface of the northern regions.

It was precisely this topic that Major Donellan and his secretary were discussing a few days later, in the darkest corner of the Two Friends tavern.

'Well!' Dean Toodrink was saying, 'Could this Barbicane – fingers crossed he is hanged one of these days! – could he be right?'

'It's likely,' replied Major Donellan, 'and I would even add that it looks certain.'

'But, then, that means there are fortunes to be won by developing the polar regions!'

'Without a doubt!' replied the major. 'Since North America already possesses vast deposits of mineral fuel, and since we so often come upon new ones, it is not unlikely that there remain some large mines to be discovered, Mr Toodrink. Now, the Arctic lands appear to form an annexe to the American continent. Note the contiguity of structure and appearance. More specifically, Greenland is an extension of the New World, and it is clear that Greenland is part of America…'

'As a horse's head – it does look rather like one – connects to the animal's body,' observed Major Donellan's secretary. 'I would add,' Toodrink went on, 'that during his expeditions in the region of Greenland, Professor Nordenskiöld noticed sedimentary formations made up of sandstone and schist with layers of lignite and containing a substantial quantity of fossilised plants. In the Diskö area alone, the Dane Stoënstrup identified seventy-one seams, full of vegetal forms: certainly vestigial signs of that flourishing vegetation that once clustered with such extraordinary luxuriance around the polar axis.'

'But further north…?' Toodrink wondered.

'Higher up, or further to the north,' the Major replied, 'the presence of coal has been physically seen and confirmed, and easily accessible too, it would seem. Therefore, if coal is so widespread along the surface of these lands, may we not almost certainly conclude that the deposits reach down right into the depths of the Earth's crust?'

Major Donellan was right. With his profound knowledge of geological formations at the North Pole, he could not help but be the most irritable of Englishmen in the circumstances. And perhaps he would have spoken on the subject at some length, had he not realized that tavern habitués were trying to overhear. So he and Dean Toodrink judged it prudent to maintain their discretion, at which, Mr Toodrink made the following last remark:

'Does one thing not surprise you, Major Donellan?'

'And what would that be?'

'That, in this business where one might expect to come across engineers, or sailors at least, since we are dealing with the North Pole and its coal reserves, instead it is artillery-men who are running the show!'

'True,' replied the Major, 'that cannot be anything but surprising!'

Still, each morning the newspapers returned to the fray, with further opinions on the subject of these coalmines…

'Coal deposits? Which would those be?' inquired the *Pall Mall Gazette*, in furious columns inspired by the high tone the English were taking in their polemics against the North Polar Exploitation Association's arguments.

'What coal deposits?' the editors of the Charleston *Daily News* shot back, being firm partisans of President Barbicane. 'Why, in the first place, the deposits that were discovered by Captain Nares in 1875–6, along latitude 84°, when he also found strata indicating the existence of a full Miocene flora, including poplars, beech, viburnam, hazelnuts and conifers.'

'And in 1881–4,' added the *New York Witness*'s science reporter, 'during Lieutenant Greely's expedition to Lady Franklin Bay, was a layer of coal not discovered by our country-men, a short distance from Fort Conger, at Watercourse Creek? And did Doctor Pavy not rightly insist that these lands are not at all lacking in carboniferous deposits, very likely planted by far-sighted Nature one day that we may combat the cold in these desolate regions?'

With such conclusive facts as these cited on the authority of the hardy American discoverers, we can see why President Barbicane's opponents could find no ready reply. So the partisans of the 'why should there be coal?' party began to give way to those adhering to the 'why shouldn't there be?' camp.

Yes, there was coal! And probably rather a lot of it. The ground around the pole was hiding great stores of the precious fuel, buried precisely in the heart of those regions where vegetation had once grown rampant.

However, if they lacked ammunition on the question of coal deposits, whose existence deep in the Arctic lands was now beyond dispute, the deniers took their revenge by approaching the question from another point of view.

'Very well!' Major Donellan concluded one day, during a discussion that he had begun in the Gun Club's own lounge and during the course of which he tackled President Barbicane as one man to another. 'Very well! I allow it; I agree, even. There is coal in the land acquired by your society. But just go and get it…!'

'That is what we shall do,' replied Impey Barbicane, calmly.

'Go beyond the 84th parallel, then, beyond which no explorer has yet set foot!'

'So we shall.'

'Go as far as the pole itself!'

'We shall go that far.'

Hearing the Gun Club's president speak so coolly, with such assurance, and his opinion asserted so openly, so decidedly, his most obstinate opponents pronounced themselves no longer sure. They felt themselves in the presence of a man who had lost none of his youthful qualities: poised, cool, his mind eminently serious and focused, as precise as a chronometer, adventurous but carrying practical ideas right through into the most daring of his enterprises…

Major Donellan stifled a wild impulse to strangle his adversary. He was robust, all right, President Barbicane, morally and physically; 'his keel ran deep', to borrow a metaphor from Napoleon, and was therefore capable of holding out come hell or high water. His enemies, those who competed with or envied him, knew it only too well.

Nevertheless, since it is impossible to stop poor jokers from telling poor jokes, this was the form chosen by those still exasperated with the new society. The most preposterous projects were attributed to the Gun Club's president. Caricature became a common resort, especially in Europe and, above all, in the United Kingdom – still struggling to digest her failure in this battle in which dollars had trounced sterling.

Ha! The Yankee had stated that he would reach the North Pole! Ha! He was planning to set foot where no other human being had yet been! Ha! He was going to plant the United States' flag on the only spot on the planet that is eternally still, while everywhere else spins on in the diurnal rotation!

At this point, the caricaturists gave themselves carte blanche.

In the windows of the major bookshops and kiosks throughout Europe's great cities, as well as in the major American towns – that freest of free countries – appeared sketches and cartoons showing President Barbicane on the hunt for the most extravagant means of reaching the pole.

One had the intrepid American, pickaxe in hand and assisted by all the Gun Club's members, digging a submarine tunnel through the mass of submerged ice, from the first floes all the way up to latitude 90° North, so as to emerge right underneath the pole.

In another, Impey Barbicane, accompanied by J-T Maston (a fine likeness) and Captain Nicholl, were coming in to land by hot-air balloon on this much-disputed stretch of ground and, following their heart-stopping bid for success, having braved a thousand dangers, the trio were celebrating victory over a lump of coal weighing all of half-a-pound. This represented the entire yield of the famous polar coal mine.

J-T Maston, too, was sketched in an issue of *Punch* magazine, being no less a target of the caricaturists' than his leader. Shown trapped in the field of the magnetic pole, the Gun Club secretary was helpless, pinned to the ground by his metal hook.

It should be mentioned that the celebrated mathematician was too short-tempered to see the funny side of any teasing that attacked his personal physique. He was extremely indignant, and Mrs Evangelina Scorbitt, as can easily be imagined, was not slow to share his indignation.

Another sketch, in the *Lanterne Magique* of Brussels, showed Impey Barbicane and the members of the society's governing board conducting a session in the midst of an inferno, like so many flame-resistant salamanders. Aiming to melt the ice of the Paleochrystic ocean, they had decided to overlay its surface with an entire sea of alcohol, then to set this sea alight – thus transforming the Polar Basin into an enormous punchbowl. Then, playing on the word 'punch', the Belgian cartoonist had taken his irreverence even further, showing the Gun Club's president in the form of a ludicrous Mr Punch.

But of all these caricatures, the most popular was that published by the French newspaper *Charivari*, from the pen of the cartoonist 'Stop'. Inside a whale's stomach, comfortably furnished and lined with cushions, Impey Barbicane and J-T Maston were sitting at a table playing chess while waiting to arrive at their destination. A pair of Jonas, the president and his secretary had not hesitated to be swallowed by the giant marine mammal: it was by this new means of locomotion that, having passed beneath the ice floes, they intended to reach the planet's unreachable pole.

The phlegmatic director of the new society was not fundamentally much perturbed by this outpouring of nib and pencil. He let the gossiping, rumour-mongering, parodies and caricatures carry on around him. He would not be deflected from the work at hand.

Indeed, being now definitively licensed to exploit the polar region, as contracted by the American government, in accordance with its board's decision, the Society had just advertised a public subscription for the sum of $15 million. Priced at $100, the shares would be released in a single payment. Such was Barbicane & Co.'s credit that subscribers poured in. But it must be added that they came, almost exclusively, from the thirty-eight states of the USA.

'All the better!' insisted champions of the North Polar Exploitation Association. 'No project could be more American!'

In short, the façade presented by Barbicane & Co. was so well constructed; the speculators believed so firmly in the eventual realization of its commercial promise; they agreed so unshakeably in the existence of coal reserves at the North Pole, as well as in the possibility of mining them, that the new society's capital was underwritten three times over.

The subscriptions, then, had to be cut by two thirds and, on the 16th December, the society's capital was finally logged as a balance of $15 million.

This was approximately three times the sum obtained by subscriptions for the Gun Club's great experimental voyage from the Earth to the Moon.

VI

IN WHICH A TELEPHONE CONVERSATION BETWEEN MRS SCORBITT AND J-T MASTON IS INTERRUPTED

Not only had President Barbicane stated that he would reach his goal – and now his capital would allow him to get there without further obstacle – but he would certainly not have dared to call on these funds if he had not been certain of success.

The North Pole would at last be conquered by man's audacious genius.

It was well known that President Barbicane and his governing board had the means to succeed where so many others had failed. They would do what neither Franklin, nor Kane, nor De Long, nor Nares, nor Greely had managed. They would go beyond the 84th parallel, they would take possession of that vast portion of the planet acquired by their final bid, they would add to the American flag the thirty-ninth star of the thirty-ninth state annexed to the American federation.

'Charlatans!' the European delegates and their Old World supporters repeated to each other.

Nothing could be more real, however, and their practical, logical, unstoppable plan for conquering the North Pole – a plan of such simplicity it might be called childish – was J-T Maston's suggestion. It was from this brain, where ideas simmered in perpetually fervescent cerebral matter, that the notion of this great geographical undertaking had sprung, along with the means of carrying it out.

It cannot be too often repeated: the Gun Club's secretary was a remarkable mathematician – we would call him 'emeritus', were the word's true meaning not diametrically opposed to the one it is accorded in common parlance. For Maston, solving the most complicated problems of mathematical science was merely a game. He laughed off the difficulties of algebra, the science of magnitudes, as he did those of arithmetic, the science of numbers. It was quite something to see him juggling those symbols, the signs gathered by convention under the rubric of algebra, whether – being alphabetical letters – they represented quantities or magnitudes, or whether – being paired or crossed lines – they indicated the relations we establish between quantities and processes we are taking them through.

Coefficients, exponents, radicals, indices and all the other rules adopted by this foreign language: how the signs danced beneath his pen, or rather beneath the stick of chalk that waggled at the end of his iron hook, for he preferred to work with a blackboard. There, on that ten-square-metre surface – no less would do for J-T Maston – he would give himself up to the passion of his algebraic nature. And he never allowed mean digits into his calculations. His were prodigious figures, monumental numbers, shaped by an ardent hand. His 2s and 3s were as plump as paper hens; his 7s were shaped like gallows, lacking only a man to hang from them; his 8s were curved like broad pairs of spectacles; his 6s and 9s signed off with interminable flourishes.

And the letters with which he wrote out his formulae: the first in the alphabet, a, b and c, that were used to represent known or given quantities, and the last, x, y and z, which he used for quantities as yet unknown or to be determined, how he made them stand out, formed from a single line, not a stroke out of place, and most especially his *zs,* which snaked in dazzling zigzags! And how finely curved his Greek letters were, his π, his λ, his ω, etc; an Archimedes or a Euclid might have shaped them.

As for the symbols, drawn in pure, unsmudged chalk, they were quite simply wonderful. His + showed admirably that this sign indicates the addition of two quantities; his −, while more modest, yet put up a fine show. His Xs rose up like Saltire crosses. As for his =, their two lines, strictly level, showed that truly J-T Maston came from a country where equality is no vain formula, at least among white men. The same grandeur of workmanship could be seen in his <, his >, his >< , all executed in quite extraordinary proportions. As for the symbol $\sqrt{}$, which denotes the root of a number or quantity, this was his crowning glory and, when he completed it with its horizontal bar, like this: $\sqrt{}$ it seemed that this meaningful arm, pointing out beyond the blackboard's edge, threatened to enthral the whole world with his impassioned equations.

Now do not imagine that J-T Maston's mathematical intelligence ended at the limits of elementary algebra. Neither differential calculus, nor integral calculus, nor the calculus of variations were foreign to him, and it was with a steady hand that he traced that famous symbol of integration, that letter, chilling in its simplicity: $\int$ the sum of an infinity of infinitely tiny elements!

The same went for the symbol Σ, which represents the sum of a finite number of finite elements, as for the symbol ∞, by which mathematicians designate infinity, and for all the mysterious symbols used in this language, incomprehensible to the common run of mortals.

In short, this amazing man would have been capable of working at the highest levels of advanced mathematics.

Such was J-T Maston. This is why his colleagues could be so confident when he took charge of solving the most preposterous calculations that their audacious brains put forward. This was what had led the Gun Club to entrust him with the problem of launching a projectile from the Earth to the Moon. And lastly, this is why Mrs Evangelina Scorbitt, enraptured by his distinction, felt an admiration for him that tended towards love.

Besides, for the case at hand – that is, for the solution to the problem of conquering the North Pole – J-T Maston would not be obliged to scale the very summits of analysis. In order to enable the new proprietors of the Arctic realm to develop it, the Gun Club's secretary faced a problem of mere mechanics – a complex problem, certainly, that would call for ingenious formulae, perhaps even brand-new ones, but from which he ought soon to emerge at the top of his game.

You could rely on J-T Maston, even though the least of errors would have led to the loss of millions. Never, since the time his childish head had tackled the first precepts of mathematics, had he made a mistake – even by a thousandth of a micron, when his calculations related to measuring a length. Had he been mistaken by even so little as the twentieth decimal place, he would not have hesitated to put a bullet in his rubber skull.

It was important to emphasize J-T Maston's remarkable ability. Now, it is time to show it at work and, to this end, we have to step back in time a few weeks.

It was about a month before the publication of the letter that J-T Maston had taken it upon himself to work through the fundamentals of the project the incredible consequences of which he had described to his colleagues.

For a number of years, J-T Maston had been living at number 179 Franklin Street, one of Baltimore's most peaceful streets, far from the business district for whose bustle he had no patience, far from the hateful noise of the crowd.

There he maintained a modest dwelling that went by the name of Ballistic Cottage, his whole fortune being only his artillery officer's pension and the stipend he received as secretary to the Gun Club. He lived alone, waited on by his negro servant Fire-Fire – 'Fire-Fire!' – a name worthy of an artillery-man's valet. But this negro was no mere servant, he was an artillery server, of the first rank, and he served his master as he had served his cannon.

J-T Maston was a confirmed bachelor, being persuaded that single life remained the only acceptable situation for him on Earth. He knew the Slavic saying: 'A woman will pull harder on a single hair than four oxen at the plough!' and he was wary.

On the other hand, if he lived a solitary life at Ballistic Cottage, that was how he wanted it. As we know, he had only to say the word to exchange his one-man solitude for a two-person solitude, and the meanness of his fortune for the riches of a millionaire. He could not doubt it: Mrs Evangelina Scorbitt would have been overjoyed to… But thus far, at least, J-T Maston would not have been overjoyed to… So it seemed clear that the two creatures, so well suited to each other – at least this was the affectionate widow's opinion – would never come to effect this transformation.

The cottage was very simple. A ground floor with veranda and one floor above. A small lounge and small dining room on the ground floor, with kitchen and pantry both housed in an adjoining building at a right angle to the small garden. Upstairs were a bedroom that looked to the street and a study that gave onto the garden, free from the hurly-burly outside. A *buen retiro* for scholar and sage, between the walls of which so many mathematical solutions had been found: it would have been the envy of Newton, Laplace and Cauchy.

What a contrast with Mrs Evangelina Scorbitt's mansion, situated in the wealthy New Park neighbourhood, its balconied façade adorned with sculptural fantasies drawn from British architecture, at once Gothic and Renaissance, its drawing rooms richly furnished, its imposing hallway, its galleries filled with paintings (the French masters in pride of place), its double staircase, its many domestics, stables, outhouses, its garden with lawns, tall trees, sparkling fountains and the tower that dwarfed all the other buildings, at the top of which fluttered the blue and gold pennant of the house of Scorbitt.

Three miles at least lay between the mansion in New Park and Ballistic Cottage. But a special telephonic line connected the two houses and, on hearing the 'Hallo? Hallo?' that heralded communication between cottage and mansion, conversation would be established. While the speakers were unable to see each other, they were able to hear everything. No reader will be surprised to learn that Mrs Evangelina Scorbitt was in the habit of calling J-T Maston from her telephone more often than J-T Maston called Mrs Evangelina Scorbitt from his. On these occasions, the mathematician would leave his work, not without some regret, hear the friendly greeting, reply with a growl whose scarcely gallant tones were, we must hope, softened by the electrical fizz, and then he would go back to his equations.

It was on the 3rd October, following one last and long meeting, that J-T Maston took leave of his colleagues and went to set about his task. This work with which he had been charged was of the utmost importance, for it was to do the calculations for all the mechanical processes that would provide access to the North Pole and thereby enable the exploitation of the deposits buried beneath its ice.

J-T Maston had estimated that it would take him about a week to accomplish his mysterious task, which was truly complex and delicate, requiring the solution of a range of equations involving mechanics, three-dimensional analytic geometry, polar geometry and trigonometry too.

In order to prevent any disturbance, it had been agreed that, while sequestered in his cottage, the Gun Club's secretary should be bothered there by nobody. Very trying for Mrs Evangelina Scorbitt; but she was obliged to be resigned to it. So it was that, when President Barbicane, Captain Nicholl, their colleagues Colonel Bloomsberry, the dashing Bilsby and the wooden-legged Tom Hunter came, during the afternoon, to pay J-T Maston one last visit, she came too.

'You shall succeed, dear Maston!' she said, when the time came for goodbyes.

'Above all, don't let's have any slip-ups!' added President Barbicane, smiling.

'Slips? He?' cried out Mrs Evangelina Scorbitt.

'Nothing worse than God's when he was devising the laws of celestial mechanics!' was the Gun Club secretary's modest reply.

Then, after handshakes from some and deep sighs from another, wishes for success and recommendations not to exhaust himself with excessive hard work, each took their leave of the mathematician. The door of Ballistic Cottage closed and Fire-Fire was ordered not to reopen it to anyone – not even to the President of the United States of America.

During the first two days of his seclusion, J-T Maston turned the problem facing him over and over in his mind without once picking up his chalk. He re-read certain works pertaining to the elements, to the Earth, its mass, density, volume, its shape, its movements of rotation upon its axis and in orbit around the Sun – subjects which must form the basis of his calculations.

Here are the main facts, of which the reader may like to be reminded.

The Earth's shape: an ellipsoid in revolution, of which the radius at its longest point is 6,377,398 metres or 1,594 leagues of 4 kilometres; at its shortest point the radius comes to 6,356,080 metres or 1,589 leagues. This, due to the flattening of our sphere at its two poles, makes for a difference between the two radii of 21,310 metres, or about 5 leagues.

The Earth's circumference at the equator: 40,000 kilometres, or 10,000 leagues of four kilometres.

The Earth's surface – at a rough estimate: 510 million square kilometres.

The Earth's volume: about 1,000 billion kilometres cubed, where each cube is 1,000 miles long, wide and high.

The Earth's density: about five times that of water, which is to say a little more than the density of heavy spar, almost that of iodine – that is, 5,480 kilograms per average metre cubed of the Earth, assuming it were weighed piece by piece, brought to the surface one after the other. This is the figure that Cavendish came to by means of the scale invented and built by Mitchell. Or, more rigorously calculated, 5,670 kilograms, following Baily's corrections. Messrs. Wilsing, Cornu, Baille, etc. have since reiterated these measurements.

Duration of the Earth's rotation around the Sun: 365 days and a quarter, constituting the solar year; or more precisely, 365 days, six hours, nine minutes, ten seconds and thirty-seven hundredths of a second – which gives our sphere a speed of 30,400 metres or seven leagues, six tenths, per second.

Speed achieved during the Earth's rotation on its axis by points lying along the Equator: 463 metres per second or 417 leagues per hour.

The following, then, constitute the units of length, force, time and angle that J-T Maston used in making his calculations: the metre, the kilogram, the second and the radian, that is, a measure of the angle formed by an arc which is equal to the radius.

It was 5th October, around five o'clock in the afternoon – it is important to be specific with such a significant project – that, after much productive thinking, J-T Maston began to write. At first, he attacked his dilemma from the bottom, that is, from the number that represents the Earth's circumference as at one of its great circles, namely the equator.

The blackboard was there, in a corner of the office, on its polished oak trestle, well lit by one of the windows that opened onto the garden. Small sticks of chalk lay waiting on the ledge fitted to the base of the board. The sponge for wiping out was within reach of the mathematician's left hand. As for his right hand, or rather his artificial hook, this was to be occupied by plotting out diagrams, formulae and figures.

Starting with an astonishingly circular line, J-T Maston drew a circumference to represent the earthly sphere. At the equator, the planet's curvature was marked by a solid line, representing the part in front of the curve, then by a dotted line, indicating the part behind – so as to convey clearly the projection of a spherical body. As for the axis running through the two poles, this was shown by a line perpendicular to the plane of the equator, labelled with the letters N and S.

Then, in the right-hand corner of the board was written this number, representing the Earth's circumference in metres:

40,000,000

This done, J-T Maston readied himself to begin his series of calculations.

He was so absorbed that he had not observed the state of the sky – which had been changing substantially during the afternoon. For the last hour, one of those great storms had been gathering whose electricity disturbs the organisms of all living things. Ashen clouds, like huge pallid blotches massed against a lead-grey sky, were rolling heavily in above the city. Far-off growls were reverberating between the resonant surfaces of Earth and Space. One or two flashes had already streaked through the air and the electrical tension was becoming unbearable.

More and more absorbed in his work, J-T Maston saw and heard nothing beyond it.

Suddenly, the abrupt tinkling of an electric bell broke his silence.

'Well!' exclaimed J-T Maston. 'When it's not by the door that unwanted visitors arrive, it's by the telephone line! A fine invention for people seeking some peace and quiet…! I shall take the precaution of disconnecting the current while I am working!'

Now, advancing on the apparatus, he wondered:

'What can they want of me?'

'Only to communicate for just a few seconds!' replied a female voice.

'And who is speaking?'

'You do not recognise me, dear Mister Maston? It is I… Mrs Scorbitt!'

'Mrs Scorbitt!… So she won't allow me even a minute's peace!'

But these last words – hardly gracious towards the amiable widow – were prudently muttered at some distance, in such a way as not to reach the telephone's metal mouthpiece.

Then, understanding that he could not avoid at least making some polite response, J-T Maston went on:

'Ah! Is it you, Mrs Scorbitt?'

'Yes, I, dear Mr Maston!'

'And what does Mrs Scorbitt want of me?'

'To warn you that a violent storm will imminently strike the city!'

'Well, I cannot stop it…'

'No, but I wanted to ask if you have taken care to close your windows…'

Mrs Evangelina Scorbitt had hardly finished the sentence when a tremendous thunderclap filled the room. It was as if a vast piece of silk were eternally tearing in two. The bolt had fallen somewhere in the vicinity of Ballistic Cottage and, conducted by the telephone wire, the flux had just burst through the mathematician's study with a purely electrical brute force.

Leaning over the mouthpiece of the telephone, J-T Maston received the most powerful electric shock that ever thumped a scholar on the chin. Then, the spark racing to earth via his iron hook, he was thrown to the floor like a paper doll. At the same time, knocked by Maston as he fell, the blackboard went flying into a corner of the room. After which, escaping through the invisible exit of a window, the lightning bolt followed a drainpipe out and down and vanished into the ground.

Stunned, J-T Maston sat up, rubbed various parts of his body, and made sure he was not injured. This done, not in the least discomposed, as you might expect from a former gun-layer of Columbiad cannon, he put everything in his study back in order, stood his trestle up again, replaced the blackboard, gathered up the pieces of chalk that scattered over the rug, and went back to his so-rudely interrupted work.

But he then saw that, following the blackboard's flight, the inscription he had made in the right-hand corner, stating the Earth's circumference at the equator in metres, had been partially rubbed out. He was therefore just beginning to restore it when the telephone rang once more with a feverish tinkling.

'Again!' roared J-T Maston.

'Who is it?' he enquired.

'Mrs Scorbitt'.

'And what does Mrs Scorbitt want of me?'

'Did that terrible thunderbolt fall upon Ballistic Cottage?'

'I have every reason to think it did!'

'Ah! Good God! The thunderbolt…!'

'Be reassured, Mrs Scorbitt!'

'You were not harmed, dear Mr Maston?'

'Not at all.'

'Are you quite certain it did not touch…'

'I am touched only by your concern on my account,' – J-T Maston felt obliged to respond gallantly.

'Good evening, dear Maston!'

'Good evening, dear Mrs Scorbitt.'

And he added, returning to his place:

'Devil take her, that excellent woman! If she had not so importunately called me to the telephone, I should not have run the risk of being struck by lightning!'

This call was the last, however; J-T Maston would not be further disturbed in the midst of his task. Besides, in order better to safeguard the peace he needed for his work, he put the telephone entirely out of action, by pulling out the electric wire.

Picking up once more from the number he had just written, he worked out the various formulae and, to conclude, one definitive formula that he noted down on the left-hand side of the board, after rubbing out all the figures that had led him to it.

Then he launched into an interminable series of algebraic signs...

A week later, on 11th October, the splendid calculation was complete, and, in triumph, the Gun Club secretary brought his colleagues the solution to the problem, for which they had naturally been waiting with great impatience.

The practical plan for reaching the North Pole in order to make use of its coal reserves was mathematically established. Hereupon, a society by the name of the North Polar Exploitation Association was founded, to which the government in Washington would grant propriety of the Arctic regions in the event that the auction resulted in their acquiring it. We know what happened next: the United States of America having won the lot at auction, the new society went on to appeal for contributions from the capitalists of both Old and New Worlds.

VII

IN WHICH PRESIDENT BARBICANE SAYS NO MORE THAN IT SUITS HIM TO SAY

On 22nd December, all Barbicane & Co.'s subscribers were invited to a general meeting, at the Gun Club's rooms in Union Square. In fact, the square itself would hardly have contained the eager crowd of shareholders. But an open-air meeting was impractical on that date, with the mercury at ten degrees below zero.

Usually, the Gun Club's vast hall was decorated with all kinds of contraptions belonging to its members' noble profession. It was a veritable museum of artillery. The bizarre appearance of the furnishings themselves, the chairs and tables, armchairs and divans, recalled those murderous machines that had sent so many brave men to a better world, though their secret hope had been to die of old age.

In any case, that day they were obliged to put away some of the jumble. This was not a council of war, but a peaceful and commercial gathering over which Impey Barbicane would preside. Much space was therefore found for the numerous subscribers who had hastened there from all corners of the United States. They huddled, crushed and choked each other in the hallway and throughout the various adjoining rooms, not to mention in the endless queue, whose excited participants trailed right out into the middle of Union Square.

Of course, the Gun Club's own members – who were also the first subscribers to the new society's shares – had places close to the table. Among them, and more jubilant than ever, could be seen Colonel Bloomsberry, wooden-legged Tom Hunter and their colleague the dashing Bilsby. Very gallantly, they had kept a comfortable armchair for Mrs Evangelina Scorbitt who, as the majority owner of the Arctic property, was quite right to take her place at President Barbicane's side. The multitude of women from all walks of Baltimore life ornamented the noisy crowd now being squeezed in beneath the hall's stained-glass dome, with the diverse bouquets, the extravagant feathers and the ribbons of every colour that graced their hats.

Overall, the great majority of the shareholders present at this meeting were not only supporters but also personal friends of members of the board.

One observation, however: the European delegates, Swedish, Danish, English, Dutch and Russian, all had seats specially assigned; their presence at the meeting was due to each man's subscribing to exactly the number of shares required to confer the right to a vote. Having been so perfectly united over the purchase, they were no less united now in their aim to discomfort the successful purchasers. We may easily imagine the intense curiosity that drove them to discover what President Barbicane was going to announce. This announcement – none doubted it – would throw light on the planned procedure for reaching the North Pole. Was this not the greater difficulty, far greater than that of extracting its coal reserves? If any objections to the procedures tabled were to occur to them, Eric Baldenak, Boris Karkof, Jacques Jansen and Jan Harald would not think twice about speaking up. For his part, Major Donellan, prompted by Dean Toodrink, was firmly intending to corner his rival Impey Barbicane; he would not give an inch.

It was eight o'clock in the evening. The hall, the lounges, the courtyards of the Gun Club were all resplendent in the light shining from their Edison chandeliers. Since the opening of the besieged doors to the public, a tumult of ceaseless murmuring had buzzed upwards from all those present. But all fell silent at the usher's announcement of the entrance of the governing board.

There, on a draped platform, in front of a table also swathed in black cloth, lit from every side, President Barbicane, the secretary J-T Maston and their colleague Captain Nicholl took their places. A triple hurrah, punctuated by grunts and hip-hips, burst along the hallway and tailed off in the adjacent streets.

Solemnly, J-T Maston and Captain Nicholl sat down, enjoying the feeling of pure celebrity.

Then, President Barbicane, who had stayed standing, put his left hand into his pocket, his right into his waistcoat, and made the following pronouncement:

'Ladies and gentlemen; subscribers all. The governing board of the North Polar Exploitation Association has called you together at the Gun Club in order to impart important information.

'You will have learnt from discussions in the newspapers that the object of our new Society is the mining of coal reserves at the Arctic pole, which region has been granted to us by the federal government. Acquired by means of public sale, this land constitutes its new owners' property in the business at hand. The capital now at their disposition following the subscription that closed on 11th December last, will allow them to organize this undertaking, the revenue of which should make profits at levels unknown to this day in any commercial or industrial operation whatsoever.'

At this, some preliminary murmurs of approval briefly interrupted the speaker.

'You will be aware,' he went on, 'that we have been led to confirm the existence of rich deposits of coal, perhaps also of fossilised ivory, in the circumpolar regions. Articles published by press around the world leave no room for doubt as to the existence of these coal deposits.

'Now, coal has become the foundation of all our modern industry. Leaving aside charcoal and coke, which are required for heating, and even ignoring coal's essential role in the production of steam and electrical power, I shall list only its derivatives: the colourings of madder, orchil, indigo, fuchsine and carmine; the flavourings of vanilla, bitter almonds, meadowsweet, cloves, wintergreen, aniseed, camphor, thymol and heliotropin, the picrates, salicylic acid, napthol, carbolic acid, antipyrine, benzine, naphthaline, pyrogallic acid, hydroquinone, tannin, saccharine, tar, asphalt, pitch, lubricating oils, polishes, prussiate of potash, cyanide, bitters, etc., etc.'

After this enumeration, the orator panted like a marathon runner stopping to catch his breath. Then, after a deep inspiration, he continued:

'It is, therefore, certain,' he said, 'that coal – this substance of the utmost preciousness – will be exhausted in a relatively short period of time due to our extravagant use of it. Within five hundred years all the coal mines currently in operation will be empty...'

'Three hundred years!' called out one of those watching.

'Two hundred!' called back another.

'Shall we say: by a more or less imminent date,' President Barbicane compromised. 'Let us then be busy seeking new sources of production, as if our coal were set to run out before the end of the nineteenth century.'

Here, a pause, encouraging his audience to listen more closely; then a resumption in these terms:

'This is why, ladies and gentlemen subscribers, you must rise up, follow me and we shall set off for the Pole!'

And indeed, the whole audience made as if to go and pack its trunks, as if President Barbicane had just unveiled their ship casting off for the Arctic regions.

Then a remark, expressed in the clear, sharp voice of Major Donellan, stopped this first impulse – as enthusiastic as it was ill-considered – in its tracks.

'Before we all set off,' he inquired, 'I should like to ask how you would go about journeying up to the pole? Are you planning to get there by sea?'

'Neither by sea, nor by land, nor by air,' replied President Barbicane, calmly.

And the gathering settled again, understandably prey to a certain curiosity.

'You will not be unaware,' the speaker continued, 'of the various attempts made at reaching this most inaccessible spot on our planet. However, I shall reprise them here in summary, as due homage to those brave pioneers who survived, as well as to those who were overcome in these superhuman trials.'

Approval was unanimous, from all the listeners, regardless of nationality.

President Barbicane began: 'In 1845, on his third voyage with the *Erebus* and the *Terror*, aiming to reach the pole, the Englishman Sir John Franklin plunges deep into the northern regions and is never heard of again.

'In 1854, the American Kane and his lieutenant Morton go in search of Sir John Franklin and, while they make it home from their expedition, their vessel the *Advance* does not.

'In 1859, the Englishman MacClintock discovers a document intimating that there has been not one survivor of the expedition led by the *Erebus* and the *Terror*.

'In 1860, the American Hayes leaves Boston on the schooner *United States*, crosses the 81st parallel, but returns in 1862 having got no further, despite the heroic efforts of his companions.

'In 1869, Captains Koldervey and Hegeman, both German, depart from Bremerhaven aboard the *Hansa* and the *Germania*. Crushed against the ice, the *Hansa* founders at a little below latitude 71° and the crew owes its salvation entirely to its lifeboats, in which they manage to regain the coast of Greenland. As for the *Germania*, more happily, she makes it back to the port of Bremerhaven, having not however pushed any further than the 77th parallel.

'In 1871, Captain Hall sets sail from New York on the steamer *Polaris*. Four months later, while enduring a difficult winter, the valiant mariner succumbs to the strain. A year later, brought down by icebergs without ever making it to latitude 84°, the *Polaris* is smashed to pieces between drifting ice floes. Having landed upon the orders of Lieutenant Tyson, the eighteen men on board are only able to make it back to land by embarking on a breakaway ice floe and abandoning themselves to the caprice of the Arctic Sea. The thirteen men to stay behind on the *Polaris* are never recovered.

'In 1875, the Englishman Nares sail from Portsmouth with the *Alert* and the *Discovery*. It is during this memorable expedition, during which the crews winter between the 82nd and 83rd parallels, that, on heading north, Captain Markham stops only four hundred miles from the Pole, no man having come so close before him.

'In 1879, our admirable citizen Gordon Bennett…'

Here three full-throated hurrahs greeted the name of that 'admirable citizen', the publisher of the *New York Herald*.

'…fits out the ship *Jeannette*, which he entrusts to Commander De Long, a gentleman of French extraction. The

Jeannette sails from San Francisco with thirty-three men, crosses the Bering Strait, is trapped in the ice up by Herald Island and founders at Bennett Island, almost bang on the 77th parallel. His men have only one course open to them: to head south, whether in the dinghies they have held on to or across the ice fields. Starvation decimates them. De Long dies in October. Many of his companions are struck down as he is and only twelve make it back from that expedition.

'Lastly, in 1881, Greely, an American, leaves the port of Saint John's in Newfoundland aboard the steamer *Proteus*, hoping to establish a camp in Lady Franklin Bay, in Grant Land, a little above the 84th parallel. Fort Conger is founded here. The hardy crew head to the west and north of the bay from this point. In 1882, Lieutenant Lockwood and his colleague Brainard reach as far as 83° 35', overtaking Captain Markham by a few miles.

'That is the furthest Northern point reached so far! It is the *Ultima Thule* of Polar cartography!'

At this: further hurrahs, and bursts of the inevitable hip-hips, in honour of the American discoverers.

'However,' President Barbicane resumed, 'their campaign was to turn out badly. The *Proteus* founders. There they are: twenty-four arctic refugees, condemned to wretched suffering. Doctor Pavy, a Frenchman, and many of the others are mortally afflicted. Rescued by the *Thetis* in 1883, Greely returns with only six of his companions. And Lieutenant Lockwood, one of the heroes of the expedition, succumbs in his turn, adding one more name to the grievous martyrology of these regions!'

This time only a respectful silence greeted the president's words, for all those present shared his understandable emotion.

Then he resumed in ringing tones:

'So it is that, despite so much determination and so much courage, no one has ever got further than the 84th parallel. We can even be confident that none ever will by the methods so far attempted, whether by ship up to the ice floes or by rafts over the ice fields. It is not for man to confront such dangers, to bear such drops in temperature. It is therefore by other means that we must seek to conquer the pole!'

From the thrill that now ran through those listening, it seemed he was coming to the heart of his speech, to the secret so dearly sought and coveted by all.

'How do you intend to go about it, then, sir?' demanded the English delegate.

'Within ten minutes you will know how, Major Donellan,' replied President Barbicane, 'and I might add, for the benefit of all our shareholders: have faith in us, for those in charge of this business are the same men who, setting off in a cylindro-conical projectile…'

'Cylindro-*comical*!' called out Dean Toodrink.

'…dared to travel right up to the Moon…'

'From where it is quite plain they found their way back again!' added Major Donellan's secretary, whose unseemly remarks provoked violent objections.

But President Barbicane shrugged and continued firmly:

'Yes, within ten minutes, ladies and gentlemen subscribers, you will know exactly what you are backing.'

A murmuring, made up of drawn-out Ohs and Ehs and Ahs, greeted this statement.

It was as if the speaker had just told his audience:

'Before ten minutes are up we shall be arriving at the pole!'

He continued with these words:

'First of all, is it a continent that forms our Earth's Arctic cap? Is it not a sea, and was Commander Nares not correct to call it the "Paleochrystic Sea", which is to say, the sea of ancient ice? To that question, I should reply: we think not.'

'That is not good enough!' shouted Eric Baldenak. 'It is not enough to "not think" it, we have to be certain…'

'Quite! And so we are, I should reply to my fiery interrupter. Yes! It is solid land, not a liquid basin, that the North Polar Exploitation Association has purchased, and which now belongs to the United States, such that no European power may ever lay claim to it!'

Muttering from the Old World delegates' benches.

'Bah! … A hole full of water… a basin… that you have no way of draining!' Dean Toodrink called out, again.

His colleagues approved, loudly.

'No, sir,' President Barbicane replied briskly. 'What we have there is a continent, a plateau raised – perhaps somewhat like the Gobi desert of Central Asia – about three or four kilometres above sea level. This was easily and logically deduced from observations made from those lands that border it, of which the polar land-mass is merely an extension. So, during their expeditions, Nordenskiöld, Peary and Maaigaard noted that Greenland slopes upwards continuously towards the North. One hundred and sixty kilometres in, counting from Diskö Island, the altitude is already 2,300 metres. Now, considering these observations, including the different products, animal and vegetable, found encased in ancient layers of ice, including the carcasses of mastodons, ivory tusks and teeth, and the trunks of conifers, we may conclude that the continent was once a fertile land, inhabited by animals certainly, by men, perhaps. There, dense forests from prehistoric times were buried, forming layers of coal, of which we are only now able to make use! Yes! It is a continent that spread out there around the Pole, a continent unblemished by any human touch and on which we are going to plant the flag of the United States of America!'

Thunderous applause.

When the last claps had faded into the far corners of Union Square, the cut-glass voice of Major Donellan could be heard to bark:

'That's seven minutes gone of the ten it was meant to take us to reach your pole…'

'We'll be there in three minutes,' replied President Barbicane coolly.

He went on:

'However, while our new property is indeed a continent, and while this continent is in fact a raised plateau, as we have reason to believe, it is nonetheless permanently obstructed by ice, covered in icebergs and ice fields, and in conditions that do appear to make access difficult.'

'Impossible!' said Jan Harald, backing his assertion with a pugnacious gesture.

'Impossible, all right,' conceded Impey Barbicane. 'Consequently, it is precisely this impossibility that we have been striving to overcome. Not only shall we require neither ships nor sledges to reach the pole, but, thanks to our procedures, ancient as well as fresh ice fields will melt as if by magic, and without costing us a single dollar of our capital, nor a minute of our labour!'

At this there was absolute silence. The 'psycho-logical' moment had come, as Dean Toodrink elegantly put it, whispering into Jacques Jansen's ear.

'Ladies and gentlemen,' the Gun Club's president went on, 'Archimedes asked only for a fulcrum and a lever to lift the

world. Well, we have found that fulcrum an
lever. We now have the capability to disp
Pole…'

'Displace the North Pole?' exclaimed Eric I

'Bring it to America!' called out Jan Harald.

President Barbicane was not inclined to exp
for the moment, because he moved on, saying:

'As for the fulcrum…'

'Don't say it! Don't say it!' called one of his a
ominous voice.

'With regard to the lever…'

'Keep your secret! Keep it!' called the majo
present.

'We will keep it!' replied President Barbicane.

You may well imagine that the European de
vexed by this reply. Despite their protests, the
intent on concealing the details of his plan. He
add:

'As for the results of the mechanical feat th
undertake and follow to its conclusion – a feat w
cedent in the history of industry: thanks to you
support – I can tell you about this straight away.'

'Listen! Listen!'

And the people listened.

'In the first place,' continued Barbicane, 'the i
for our project was conceived by one of our most
devoted and illustrious colleagues. To him, also, th
of having made the calculations that enable us to m
theory to practice for, while extracting the Arctic coal
should be child's play, shifting the Pole was a prob
only top-flight engineering could solve. This is
turned to the Gun Club's worthy secretary, J-T Masto

Hurrah! Hip… hip… hurrah! For J-T Maston!' roared the whole room, electrified by the presence of that eminent and extraordinary person.

How the applause that now burst out around the celebrated mathematician moved Mrs Evangelina Scorbitt, and how her heart was deliciously stirred!

The gentleman himself modestly made do with nodding gravely to the right, then to the left, and acknowledged his enthusiastic public with a single, raised finger.

'My dear subscribers,' Barbicane went on, 'during the great gathering we held to celebrate the arrival of the Frenchman Michel Ardan in America, some months before our departure for the Moon…' (The American referred so casually to this journey, as if it had been merely from Baltimore to New York) '…our J-T Maston said "Let us invent machines to move the North Pole, let us find our fulcrum and we shall set the Earth's axis straight!" Well, all those listening to me here, let me tell you now! The machines have been invented; the fulcrum is found; it is now to the re-alignment of the Earth's axis that we must address our efforts!'

At this, there were several minutes of stupefied silence that, in France, would be understood by that vulgar but accurate expression: 'That's a bit steep!'

'What! You dare to claim you will realign our axis?' spluttered Major Donellan.

'Yes, sir,' replied President Barbicane, 'or rather, we have the means to create a new axis, upon which diurnal rotation will take place from then on…'

'Alter the diurnal rotation…!' echoed Colonel Karkov, his eyes flashing.

'Absolutely, and without affecting its duration!' replied President Barbicane. 'Our operation will move the current

pole about as far as the 67th parallel and, in these conditions, the Earth will behave like the planet Jupiter, whose axis is almost perpendicular to the plane of its orbit. Now, this displacement of twenty-three degrees will suffice to furnish our polar property with enough warmth to melt the ice that has accumulated there over centuries!'

The audience was astounded. Nobody interrupted the speaker – not even to cheer. All were in thrall to this idea, at once so ingenious and so simple: to alter the axis upon which the earth spins.

As for the European delegates, they were quite simply dumbstruck, crushed, annihilated, and they said nothing, totally bewildered.

But the applause rang out loud enough to blow off the roof, when President Barbicane came to this sublimely simple conclusion:

'Thus the Sun itself will be responsible for melting the icebergs and floes; the Sun alone will make reaching the North Pole as easy as pie!'

'So,' asked Major Donellan, 'since man cannot go to the pole, the pole is going to come to him…?'

'You said it!' President Barbicane replied.

VIII

THE PRESIDENT OF THE GUN CLUB
SAID 'JUST LIKE JUPITER'?

During that memorable gathering in honour of Michel Ardan
– quite appropriately recalled by the speaker – if J-T Maston
had excitedly cried 'Let us shift the Earth's very axis!' this
was because the daring and eccentric Frenchman, one of the
heroes of *Journey from the Earth to the Moon* and close
colleague to President Barbicane and Captain Nicholl, had
just sung a hymn of praise in honour of our solar system's
greatest planet.

According to the solution arrived at by the Gun Club's
mathematician, a new rotational axis would replace the old
one, upon which the Earth had turned 'since the World began',
as the popular saying goes. Moreover, the new axis would
be perpendicular to the plane of the Earth's orbit. In these
circumstances, the former North Pole's new climate would
exactly match current conditions in Trondheim, Norway, in the
spring. Its paleochrystic coat of armour would therefore melt
naturally in the Sun's rays. At the same time, our climatic
modulations would take on the same distribution around the
Earth as is currently found on the surface of Jupiter.

Indeed, the incline of that planet's axis, or in other words,
the angle between its axis of rotation and the plane of its
ecliptic, is 88°13'. One degree and forty-seven minutes more,
and that axis would be exactly perpendicular to the plane of its
orbit around the Sun.

Besides – and this point bears close attention – the effort
that Barbicane & Co.'s society would deploy to modify the
Earth's actual orientation, would not, properly speaking, be

directed at repositioning its axis. According to Newtonian mechanics, no force, however great, could be made to produce such a result. The Earth is not like a fat hen on a roasting spit, rotating on a physical axis that we can take in one hand and reposition as we please. Yet, the fact is a new axis could be created – we might even say: easily – as soon as the fulcrum dreamed of by Archimedes, and the lever envisaged by J-T Maston, were made available to these audacious engineers.

Still, since the latter seemed determined to keep their invention secret until further notice, the public had to make do with debating the consequences.

This is what the newspapers and magazines did first of all, reminding those who knew, and informing the ignorant, of the effects on Jupiter of its axis' near-perpendicularity to the plane of its orbit.

Jupiter, a planet in the solar system just like Mercury, Venus, Earth, Mars, Saturn, Uranus and Neptune, travels round at about 600 million miles from their shared focus, its volume being about 1,300 times that of the Earth.

Now, if 'Jovian' life exists, if there are creatures subsisting on Jupiter's surface, then living there brings the following benefits to its inhabitants – benefits so extravagantly demonstrated at that memorable gathering that had preceded the journey to the Moon.

In the first place, during Jupiter's diurnal revolution – which takes only nine hours and fifty-five minutes – the days remain equal to the nights in every latitude; that is, four hours, 57.5 minutes for the day and four hours, 57.5 minutes for the night.

'There, you see,' believers in Jovian life observed, 'so convenient for people of regular habits. They will be delighted to live in such regularity!'

Well, this is what would happen on Earth if President Barbicane's project were a success. Only, since the speed of rotation along the Earth's new axis would be neither increased nor reduced, and since twenty-four hours would always come between one high noon and the next, the nights and days would be exactly twelve hours long at any point on the planet. Our dusks and dawns would lengthen the days by exactly equal amounts. We would live in the midst of a perpetual equinox, such as currently happens only on 21st March and 21st September in all earthly latitudes, when our radiant star appears to fit her path to the line of the equator.

'But the strangest climatic phenomenon – perhaps the most interesting too,' added the enthusiasts, 'will be the abolition of the seasons!'

Indeed, it is thanks to the axial tilt relative to the orbital plane that we have these annual variations, known by the names of spring, summer, autumn and winter. But Jovians know nothing of seasons. Therefore, Earth people, too, will leave these behind. From the moment that the new axis stands perpendicular to the ecliptic, there will be no more frigid zones, nor any torrid zones; instead, the whole Earth will enjoy temperate climes.

This is why:

The torrid zone is that part of the planet's surface that lies between the tropics of Cancer and Capricorn. All parts of this Zone are lucky enough to pass before the Sun twice a year at their zenith, while for areas within the tropics, this phenomenon occurs only once a year.

The temperate zones are the two areas that include all land situated between the tropics and the polar circles, so between 23°28' and 66°72' latitude, where the Sun never appears at its zenith, yet still shows above the horizon every day.

The frigid zones are those circumpolar regions that the Sun abandons completely for a period of time, which, for the pole itself, can be as long as six months of the year.

Understandably, one consequence of the range of heights the Sun may reach above the horizon is that the torrid zone suffers from excessive heat, while the warmth becomes moderate, if variable, the further behind we leave the tropics and move into the temperate zones, while the frigid zones experience extreme cold from the polar circles up to the poles.

On the Earth's surface with the newly perpendicular axis, it would no longer work like this. The Sun would remain immovably in line with the equator. Throughout the year, it would follow its twelve-hour course imperturbably, climbing to a distance from the zenith equal to each place's latitude, therefore higher up, the nearer each place were to the equator. So, for countries located at 20° latitude, it would rise each day to 70° above the horizon; for countries at 49°, as high as 41°; and for places on the sixty-seventh parallel, only as high as 23°. The days would then display a perfect regularity, synchronised with the Sun, which would rise and set every twelve hours at the same point on the horizon.

'Imagine the improvement!' President Barbicane's friends said to one another. 'According to his temperament, each person could reliably choose the climate that would best suit his cold turns or his hot flushes, upon a planet where the variations in temperature that are currently so troublesome would be unknown!'

In short, Barbicane & Co., those modern Titans, would change the state of things that had existed since the time when our planet, its orbit ever aslant, became the Earth we know today.

It is true that the most observant would miss a few of the stars and constellations they were used to finding in their night skies.

Poets would no longer have winter's long nights nor summer's long days to capture in their modern verses complete with the richest of rhymes. But overall, what an improvement for the majority of humankind!

'Moreover,' added those newspapers supporting President Barbicane, 'since agricultural production will become more regular, agronomists will be able to provide each vegetable species with its ideal environment.'

'That's all fine!' retorted hostile newspapers, 'but we shall always have rain, hail, gales, cyclones, thunderstorms and all those disruptions that can so seriously compromise a harvest and the fortunes of its farmers.'

'Of course,' replied the chorus of friends, 'but these disasters should become rarer thanks to the more stable climate. Humanity will do well out of this new world order. And it *will* mean the transformation of our very planet. By abolishing these troublesome seasonal variations, along with the old unequal days and nights, Barbicane & Co. will have rendered a service to present and future generations. Yes, as Michel Ardan said, our planet, the surface of which is always either too cold or too hot, will no longer be the planet of coughs and colds and bronchial malaise. No one shall have a cold apart from those who expressly want one, since those people will always have the option of moving to a country better suited to their particular bronchi.'

And, in its issue of 27th December, the *New York Sun* concluded the most eloquent of these articles with the rousing cry:

'Every honour to President Barbicane and his colleagues! Not only will these brave men effectively have annexed a new province to the American continent, and in so doing increased the already vast extent of the United States, but they will have made the whole Earth more hygienic for her inhabitants, as well as more productive, for we shall be able to sow as soon as we have reaped and, the seeds sprouting without delay, there will be no more time lost through winter. Not only will the coal mines' wealth be tapped, thus guaranteeing our supply of this indispensable commodity for what may be many years to come, but our planet's climatic conditions will be modified to everyone's advantage. Barbicane and his colleagues will have transformed our Creator's great work for the greater good of their fellow men. All credit to these men, who will take first place among the benefactors of humanity!'

IX

IN WHICH WE SENSE
THE APPROACH OF A DEUS EX MACHINA
MADE IN FRANCE

Those, then, would be the benefits of the modification to the Earth's axis to be brought about by President Barbicane. Moreover, we know that this change would only imperceptibly affect the movement of our planet around the Sun. The Earth would continue to follow its immutable orbit through Space and the conditions of the solar year would not change at all.

When the likely consequences of shifting the axis were brought to the attention of the rest of the world, there was an extraordinary outcry. At first, this advanced engineering project was received with enthusiasm. The idea of having one constant, ongoing season, depending on one's latitude – and that to be decided according to each customer's preference – was extremely attractive. People were ecstatic at the thought that every mortal would soon enjoy the same eternal spring that Telemachus' minstrel described as reigning on Calypso's island, and that they would even be able to choose between a cool spring and a warm one. As for the position of the new axis to which the diurnal rotation would shift, that was a secret that neither President Barbicane, nor Captain Nicholl, nor J-T Maston seemed willing to share. Would they reveal it beforehand, or would people know it only after the completion of the project? This question was important enough to cause serious concerns.

One thought naturally concerned many and was much discussed in the newspapers. By what mechanical means would the shift be effected, since it clearly required the deployment of an immense force?

Indeed the *Forum*, an influential New York magazine, made the following apt remarks:

'If the Earth did not already turn upon an axis, perhaps it would require some relatively weak blow to impel it into rotation around an arbitrarily chosen axis. But the Earth may be compared to an enormous gyroscope moving at a high speed, and the laws of nature demand that such a device will tend to continue turning at a constant rate on the same axis. Léon Foucault has physically demonstrated this in well-known experiments. It therefore appears very difficult, not to say impossible, to make the Earth deviate.'

A fair point. And that said, having considered what means the North Polar Exploitation Association could be thinking of, it was no less interesting to consider whether this force would be brought to bear gradually or suddenly. If the latter, would there not be frightening natural disasters along the planet's surface, at the moment when the axial change occurred, thanks to Barbicane & Co.'s procedures?

There was plenty in this to worry the scholars of Old and New Worlds as much as it did the ordinary people. All in all, a blow is a blow, and it is never agreeable to experience a blow or even the recoil from one. It appeared that the organizers of this business had not given a thought to the disruption that their project might cause to our unfortunate planet, being blinded by its benefits. So it happened that, annoyed more than ever by their defeat and determined to turn the situation to their own account, the European delegates very cleverly began to turn public opinion against the Gun Club's president.

It was the case that, having staked no claim to the circumpolar territory, France had not figured among the European Powers taking part in the auction. Nevertheless, while his country remained officially uninvolved in the affair, a Frenchman had decided to come to Baltimore, on his own account and out of personal interest, in order to follow the various phases of this prodigious enterprise.

This man was a thirty-five-year-old engineer at the Corps des Mines. Top of his class on entering this famous Ecole Polytechnique and top when he left, he was an outstanding mathematician, superior to J-T Maston, who, while himself a remarkable calculator, was *only* a calculator – as Le Verrier must appear next to Laplace, or next to Newton.

This engineer was – and this no flaw of character – a man of wit, of imagination, an original such as may occasionally turn up in Bridges, but very rarely in Mines. He had his own particularly amusing way of saying things. When he was chatting among friends, even when the subject was science, he would talk with all the abandon of a Paris street urchin. He loved the language of the street, those expressions so arbitrarily waved in and out by fashion. In his moments of leisure, you might think his style hardly suited to juggling academic formulae; indeed he was only resigned to it when sat down, pen in hand. He was also a tenacious worker, able to stay ten hours at his desk, writing fluent pages of algebra as you might write a letter. His favourite relaxation, after a long hard day of advanced mathematics, was whist, at which he was a mediocre player, despite having pre-calculated all the probabilities.

This singular character was called Alcide Pierdeux and, with his mania for abbreviation – shared, by the way, with all his friends – he generally signed himself APerd, or even AP_1, thereby avoiding ever dotting his i's. He was so fiery in arguments that he was nicknamed Sulphuric Alcide. Not only was he tall but he appeared 'lofty'. His friends agreed that his height equalled one five-millionth of a quarter-meridian, which is about two metres, and they were not wrong by much. Although his head was a little small for his powerful chest and broad shoulders, he deployed it with spirit, and what lively looks his blue eyes darted through his pince-nez! He had one of those distinctive faces that can be gay and yet grave at the same time, despite his scalp's premature baldness due to excessive indulgence in algebraic symbols beneath the glow of the study-hall gas-lamps. And with all that, he was the best student in living memory at the Ecole, and without a shadow of self-importance. Even though he was by nature rather independent, he had always bowed to the prescriptions of Code X, which dictates the rules for all the Polytechnique students, for everything to do with friendship and respect for the profession. It was adhered to as much beneath the trees in the 'Acas' quad, so-called because there were no acacias in it, as in the dormitories – where the signal tidiness of Alcide's quarters, the order that reigned in his 'lock-up', denoted an absolutely methodical mind.

But if Alcide Pierdeux's head appeared a little small at the summit of his long body, so what? In any case, his grey cells was full to bursting, of that we may be sure. He was, above all, a mathematician, as all his fellows were or had been; but he practised mathematics only so as to apply it in experimental science, which in itself held no charm for him unless it found some use in industry. This was, he well knew, a less worthy side of his nature. No one is perfect. In summary, his specialty was the study of those sciences which, despite many vital steps forward, have and will always retain secrets from those who work in them.

We should mention in passing that Alcide Pierdeux was a bachelor. As he himself would say, he was still 'equal to one', even though his dearest wish was to be doubled. In view of this, his friends had already thought of marrying him to a charming, gay and witty young woman from Martigues in Provence. Unfortunately there was a father who had responded to their first overtures with the following '*Martigalade*':

'No! Your Alcide is much too learned! The conversation he'll be troubling my poor poppet with will be quite incomprehensible to her!'

As if every true scholar were not modest and plain-speaking.

This is why, greatly vexed, our engineer had resolved to put a decent stretch of sea between himself and Provence. He applied for a year's sabbatical, was granted it, and felt he could not use it better than by going to observe the affair of the North Polar Exploitation Association. This is why he had then appeared in the United States.

Now, since Alcide Pierdeux's arrival in Baltimore, Barbicane & Co.'s great project had been a constant source of preoccupation. That the Earth might turn Jovian through a modification to its axis didn't bother him at all. But the means by which this could occur; it was this that excited the scholar's curiosity – not unreasonably.

In his picturesque style, he said to himself:

'Obviously President Barbicane is winding up to thump our ball with a top-notch wallop! ... How and in what direction? ... That says it all! ... Blimey! I can just see him give it a bit of side, like a billiard ball, when you want to add some spin! ... If he hits us full-ball, we'll be shot right out of orbit and to the devil with our beloved seasons, years, the whole caboodle; we'll bounce right off the table! No! These fine people can of course only be thinking of substituting a new axis for our old one! ... Not a doubt about it. ... But I cannot very well see where they'll set up their fulcrum, nor what shock they mean to bring in from outside! ... Ah, if we hadn't this diurnal rotation, a flick would do the job! ... Yet, we do have it, diurnal rotation! ... You can't get away from diurnal rotation: that's the very *frictionum* of it!'

He meant the 'rub', our bedazzling Pierdeux.

'In any case,' he added, 'whatever way they attack it, it'll be a right dust-up!'

All in all, however hard our scholar pounded those brain cells of his, he could not begin to imagine the method dreamed up by Barbicane and Maston. Which was all the more unfortunate for, had he known the method, he would have worked through all the mechanical calculations in the blink of an eye.

And this is why, on the day of 29th December, Alcide Pierdeux, engineer in the national corps of the Mines de France, was, to the full stretch of his long legs, pacing the busy streets of Baltimore.

X

IN WHICH A FEW ANXIETIES BEGIN TO SURFACE

It was now a month since the general meeting held in the Gun Club's rooms. During this period, public opinion had altered noticeably. The advantages of shifting the rotational axis were forgotten, while the disadvantages were beginning to be appreciated quite distinctly. It was impossible that some catastrophe would not follow, for the change in axis would have to be created by a violent impact. But the exact nature of this catastrophe remained uncertain. As for the improvement in climate; was that really so desirable? Only Eskimos, Laplanders, Samoyeds and Chukchis stood to benefit, since they had nothing to lose.

The loudest voices now against the project were those of the European delegates. To start with, they had sent reports to their governments; they had filled the transatlantic cable with their incessant traffic of dispatches; they had asked for and received instructions, the usual diplomacy-speak with its clichéd phrases: 'Show great enthusiasm, but do not compromise your government!' 'Be resolute, but do not interfere with the status quo!'

Now, Major Donellan and his colleagues continued their protests in the names of their threatened native countries.

'Indeed, it is quite clear,' Colonel Boris Karkov said, 'that the American engineers must have made sure to spare the United States as far as possible from the effects of the impact!'

'But is that possible?' responded Jan Harald. 'When harvesting olives, if you shake the olive tree, don't you expect all the branches to start quivering?'

'And if you are punched in the chest,' Jacques Jansen added, 'doesn't your whole body go flying?'

'This must be the significance of the mysterious clause in the letter!' exclaimed Dean Toodrink. 'This is why it mentioned "geographical or meteorological" modifications to the Earth's surface!'

'Yes!' cried Eric Baldenak, 'and if so, we must fear first that the shifting of the axis will flush the seas out of their natural basins.'

'And if the ocean level drops at different points,' Jacques Jansen observed, 'surely it will mean that some people will find themselves living at such heights that all communication with their fellows will have become impossible?'

'If they aren't propelled into strata where the air is so thin,' added Jan Harald, 'that they can no longer breathe!'

'Imagine London as high as Mont Blanc!' exclaimed Major Donellan.

And, standing there, legs apart and head thrown back, the gentleman gazed up at the zenith, as if the capital of the United Kingdom were there, lost among the clouds.

All considered, there was a real public danger, which became clearer as people understood the possible consequences of shifting the axis.

In fact, the axial shift would be a dramatic 23° 28', a change that would considerably displace the seas, due to the flatter parts of the planet being still at the sites of the former poles. The Earth could be at risk of disasters like those believed recently to have played out on the surface of Mars. There, whole continents, including Schiaparelli's Libya, have been submerged – as shown by the dark blue shade that has replaced the formerly reddish tint. Here, Lake Moeris vanished; there, 600,000 square kilometres of northern land have been reshaped, while to the south, the oceans have abandoned broad areas that they used to cover. And, although some charitable souls had expressed concern for the 'flood victims of Mars' and suggested organizing a subscription for them, how would it be when the time came to worry about the Earth's own flood victims?

So protests began to be heard from all quarters, and the United States government was called on to account for itself. On the whole, it seemed safer not to attempt the experiment than to risk the disasters it would surely entail. The Creator had done a good job. No need to go making foolhardy adjustments to his masterpiece.

But not everyone took it seriously. There were people out there who were flippant enough to joke about such serious things.

'Look at these Yanks!' they said to each other. 'Trying to cook our old Earth on a new rotisserie! It might be necessary if, having turned on the current one for millions of centuries, the bearings had begun to wear out, just as we change the axle on a pulley or a wheel. But our axis is surely in as perfect condition as in the very first days of creation.'

In the midst of all these recriminations, Alcide Pierdeux was trying to discover the nature and the direction of the impact planned by J-T Maston, and also the precise point on the planet where it might be produced. Once he knew this, he would be able to determine where on Earth people were truly at risk.

As we've seen, the Old World's fears were not shared by the New. It seemed that, although they were Americans, President Barbicane, Captain Nicholl and J-T Maston had not even considered how they might save the United States from the immersions that would be caused by the axial shift in various parts of Europe, Asia, Africa and Oceania. Clearly, they must have believed the stretch of the New World that lay between the Arctic regions and the Gulf of Mexico would have nothing to fear from the forthcoming jolt. They might even have thought that America would benefit from some considerable increase in its territories. Indeed, who knows if, by extending across those basins soon to be abandoned by the two oceans that currently fill them, she might not annex as many new states again as could already be counted in stars among the folds of her flag?

'Yes, of course! But,' chorused fearful people – those who see only the dangerous side of things – can one be sure of anything these days? What if J-T Maston made a mistake in his calculations? And what if President Barbicane were to make a mistake when he puts them into action? It can happen to the most skilful sharpshooters. They might not hit the target with the bullet, or remember to put the shell into the cannon.

Of course, the delegates of the European powers carefully fanned such anxieties. The secretary Dean Toodrink published several articles to this end, among his most vehement in the *Standard*, while Jan Harald published in the Swedish paper *Aftenbladet* and Colonel Boris Karkof in the widely-read Russian paper *Novoie-Vremia*. Even in America, opinion was divided. If, being liberals, the Republicans maintained their support for President Barbicane, the Democrats, as conservatives, came out against him. Some of the American press, principally the *Boston Journal*, the *New York Tribune*, etc., joined their voices to those of the European papers. Since the creation of Associated Press and United Press, the North American newspaper has become an outstanding source of public influence, paying more than $20 million a year for local and foreign news.

In vain, then, did other newspapers – no less well distributed – try to strike back in favour of the North Polar Exploitation Association. In vain did Mrs Evangelina Scorbitt offer ten dollars per line for authoritative critiques, imaginative articles and witty columns refuting the dangers as fanciful. In vain did this passionate widow seek to show that, if ever there was a ridiculous idea, it was that J-T Maston could make a mistake in his calculations. At last, paralysed by fear, little by little, America moved towards complete agreement with the Europeans.

Neither President Barbicane, nor the Gun Club's secretary, nor even the members of the governing board took the least trouble to reply to the negative coverage. They let the criticisms go on unchecked and changed nothing. They did not even show any signs of the immense preparations their great project ought to require. And that clearly wasn't because they were preoccupied with counteracting the widespread disapproval currently gaining ground over their project that had at first been welcomed with such enthusiasm.

Soon, despite Mrs Evangelina Scorbitt's dedication, however great the sums she spent defending them, President Barbicane, Captain Nicholl and J-T Maston were transformed into persons representing a risk to national security in both Old and New Worlds. The federal government was officially called by the European Powers to intervene in the affair and question the leaders of the project. They were required to make their methodology public, to state by what means they intended to replace the old axis with a new one – so that the likely consequences for public safety could be assessed – and finally, to indicate which parts of the planet would be directly threatened; in short, to reveal all that the public agitation failed to expose, and everything that prudence wished to know.

President Washington's government needed no persuading. The panic that had swept through the northern, central and southern states of his country left no room for hesitation. A research commission, made up of mechanical and geotechnical engineers, mathematicians, hydrographers and geographers, a total of fifty experts, led by the renowned John H. Prestice, was created by decree on 19th February, with full powers to call the society to account and, if necessary, to ban its project.

First of all, President Barbicane was summoned to appear before the commission.

President Barbicane did not appear.

Agents were sent to fetch him from his private apartments at 95 Cleveland Street in Baltimore.

President Barbicane was no longer there.

Where was he?

Nobody knew.

When had he gone?

Five weeks earlier, on 11th January, he had left Maryland in the company of Captain Nicholl.

Where had they both gone?

Nobody could say.

Clearly, the two Gun Club members were making their way to the mysterious region where preparations would begin under their supervision.

But where might this place be?

Understandably, there was a strong interest in discovering it, in order to nip these dangerous plans in the bud, while there was still time.

There was widespread shock at the disappearance of President Barbicane and Captain Nicholl. Soon, a flood of fury was mounting like a spring tide, threatening the directors of the North Polar Exploitation Association.

There was, however, one man who should be able to reveal where President Barbicane and his colleague had gone. One man might conclusively reply to the gigantic question mark that hovered in minds the world over.

That man was J-T Maston.

J-T Maston was summoned before the Commission of Inquiry on the orders of John H. Prestice.

J-T Maston did not appear.

Had he too left Baltimore? Had he joined his colleagues to help them in their project, the outcome of which the whole world was anticipating with such understandable horror?

In fact, J-T Maston was still living at Ballistic Cottage, no. 109 Franklin Street, working ceaselessly, already pleasantly absorbed in yet more calculations, breaking off only for the occasional evening spent in Mrs Evangelina Scorbitt's salons at the sumptuous New Park mansion.

An agent was therefore dispatched by the head of the commission with orders to bring him in.

The agent arrived at the cottage, knocked on the door, let himself into the hall, was rather rudely received by the negro servant Fire-Fire, then even more rudely by the master of the house.

Nevertheless, J-T Maston felt obliged to respect the summons, although, once in the commissioners' presence, he made no attempt to conceal his deep irritation at this interruption of his customary work.

The first question was: did the Gun Club's secretary know where President Barbicane and Captain Nicholl were currently to be found?

'I know,' replied J-T Maston firmly, 'but I don't believe I am authorized to say.'

Second question:

Were his two colleagues busy with the necessary preparations for this project of shifting the Earth's axis?

'That,' responded J-T Maston, 'is part of the secret I am compelled to keep, and I refuse to reply.'

Would he then be willing to explain his work to the Commission of Inquiry, which would decide whether to allow the society to carry out its plans?

'No, certainly not, I shall not explain it! ... I'd burn it first! ... It is my right as a free citizen of free America to explain my discoveries to nobody!'

'But if that is your right, Mr Maston,' said President John H. Prestice gravely, as if he were speaking on behalf of the whole world, 'perhaps it is your duty to speak in view of the depth of public sentiment, to put an end to the turmoil among the Earth's peoples?'

J-T Maston did not believe this to be his duty. He had only one duty: not to speak; he would not speak.

Despite their pressing, their pleading, even despite their threats, the Commission of Inquiry's panel was unable to draw anything from the man with the iron hook. You would never guess that such unbudging obstinacy might reside within a rubber skull!

J-T Maston went, then, just as he had come, and, if he were congratulated on his brave stance by Mrs Evangelina Scorbitt, there is no need to dwell on it.

When the outcome of J-T Maston's appearance before the commission was known, the public indignation took forms that genuinely threatened the retired artillery-man's security. So violent was the outcry from both European delegates and the public, and then so great the pressure upon the federal government's highest representatives that Minister of State

John S. Wright had to ask his colleagues for authorization to use force if necessary.

One evening – it was 13th March – J-T Maston was in his office in Ballistic Cottage, deep in his figures, when the telephone rang out frantically.

'Hello! … Hello! …' the receiver mumbled, vibrating with an agitation that indicated extreme disquiet.

'Who is speaking?' J-T Maston asked.

'Mrs Scorbitt.'

'And what can I do for Mrs Scorbitt?'

'Be on your guard! I have just been informed this very evening that…'

Her words had not even reached J-T Maston's ears when the door of Ballistic Cottage was rudely battered down by somebody's shoulder.

There was an extraordinary commotion on the stairs leading up to his office. A voice was pleading for mercy. Other voices were trying to silence the first. Then, the noise of a body falling.

It was the servant Fire-Fire, tumbling down from step to step, having tried in vain to defend his master's home against the assailants.

A second later, the office door was reduced to splinters and a constable appeared, followed by a squad of officers.

The constable was under orders to carry out a search at the cottage, to seize J-T Maston's papers and apprehend his person.

Incandescent, the secretary of the Gun Club snatched up a revolver and threatened the officers.

A moment later, facing unequal odds, he was disarmed and dispossessed of all the papers, densely filled with formulae and figures, that had been piled upon his table.

All at once, breaking loose with a sharp twist, J-T Maston managed to seize the notebook that contained all his calculations.

The officers leapt forward to snatch it back from him but J-T Maston managed to open it, tear out the last page and swallow it as if it were a simple pill.

'Come and take it now!' he cried, like another Leonidas at Thermopylae.

An hour later, J-T Maston was incarcerated in Baltimore jail.

And it was doubtless the best thing that could have befallen him, for – sadly for him – the public would have attacked him with such violence that the police would have been powerless to prevent them.

XI

WHAT IS AND WHAT IS NO LONGER
IN J-T MASTON'S NOTEBOOK

The notebook seized by the Baltimore police contained thirty-odd pages, dense with scribbled formulae and equations and, towards the end, with numbers summarizing the results of all J-T Maston's calculations. It represented a triumph in high-level mechanics, only fully appreciable by high-level mathematicians. It even included the 'active forces' equation:

$$\tfrac{1}{2}\left(v^2 - v_0^2\right) = gr\left\{\tfrac{r}{x} - 1 + \tfrac{m'}{m}\left(\tfrac{r}{d-x} - \tfrac{r}{d-r}\right)\right\}$$

that had come up in the calculations for *From the Earth to the Moon**, which also included mathematical expressions relating to lunar gravity.

Since the man in the street would not have understood a word of this work, it seemed appropriate to publicize these data and the results about which the whole world had been so anxious for the last few weeks.

This, then, was what the newspapers were given to propagate, as soon as the commission's experts had been informed of the famous mathematician's formulae. This, regardless of party allegiance, is what all the newspapers brought to the people's attention.

There didn't seem any point in disputing J-T Maston's work. They say that a problem correctly articulated is already halfway to resolution, and this was a remarkable case in point. The calculations had been done with such precision that

---

* [Jules Verne novel. Original French title: *De la terre à la lune*, 1865.]

the commission never questioned their accuracy or their implications. It was apparent that if the plan were carried through, the Earth's axis would be irreversibly altered, and the anticipated catastrophes would happen, in all their horror.

A communiqué from the Baltimore Commission of Inquiry, to be released to the newspapers, reviews and magazines of both Old and New Worlds:

The effect sought by the North Polar Exploitation Association's governing board, whose object is to substitute a new rotational axis for our old one, is to be obtained by means of the recoil of a device fixed at a predetermined point on the Earth. If the central bore of the device is immovably welded to the ground, it is highly likely that it will communicate its recoil down into the mass of our entire planet.

The device adopted by the society's engineers is nothing other than a colossal cannon, which would have no effect if it were to be shot straight upwards, but which, to produce the maximum effect, has to be aimed horizontally pointing either north or south. The latter direction is the one chosen by Barbicane & Co., and in these conditions, the recoil will cause a shock to the north of the planet – an impact comparable to that on a billiard ball hit very fine.

(Indeed, this was exactly what the farsighted Alcide Pierdeux had predicted.)

As soon as the shot is fired, the Earth's centre will be displaced in a direction parallel to that of the shot, which could then alter the plane of the Earth's orbit and consequently the length of our year, but to such a minimal degree that this must be considered negligible. Simultaneously, the Earth will begin rotation around an axis along the same plane as the equator; its rotation being set to continue indefinitely along this new axis, as if our former diurnal rotation had never existed prior to the impact.

Now, this movement will be pursued along the axis of the poles and, combining with the additional rotation lent by the recoil, it will bring about a brand-new axis, whose North Pole will lie at a quantity x distance from the former pole. Moreover, if the shot were fired so as to coincide with the moment when the spring equinox – one of the two annual times of intersection between the equator and the ecliptic – is at the nadir of the firing line, and if the recoil were powerful enough to displace the former pole by 23°28', the Earth's new axis would end up perpendicular to the plane of its orbit – more or less as is the case for the planet Jupiter.

We know what the consequences of this new perpendicularity would be, for President Barbicane announced them in his session of 22nd December.

However, given the Earth's mass and the speed at which it moves, is it even possible that a firearm exists of such mass that its recoil would be able to produce a shift in the position of the present pole, more particularly, a shift as great as 23°28'?

We answer 'Yes' if a cannon or series of cannon were to be built to the dimensions required for the task by the laws of mechanics, or if, not attaining those dimensions, the cannon's inventors were to possess an explosive of such force that it could endow the projectile with the speed required to achieve such a shift.

Now, if we consider a standard 27cm, French navy cannon (1875 model), which can propel a 180kg projectile at a speed of 150m per second, by increasing this gun's dimensions a hundred-fold, that is, by increasing its volume a million times, we would make it capable of launching a projectile of 180 tonnes. What's more, if the powder were to impose sufficient force to lend the projectile a speed 5,600 times greater than that of ordinary gunpowder, the desired result would be achieved. Indeed, with a speed of 2,800km per second, we would no longer need to fear that, were it to fall back to Earth again, the impact of the projectile could return everything to its initial state.

Unfortunately for our terrestrial security and as extraordinary as it might sound, J-T Maston and his colleagues have in their possession precisely that explosive of almost unlimited power. The power of the powder used to launch the cannonball and the *Columbiad* itself up to the Moon for their previous exploit pales in comparison. Captain Nicholl has discovered the new powder. As to its composition, J-T Maston's notebook gives incomplete information; he refers to the explosive only as the 'dyna-mix'.

All we know is that it is formed by the reaction of a mixture of organic compounds with azotic acid. A certain number of free radicals are substituted for the same number of hydrogen atoms, from which is obtained a powder that is formed, like pyroxile, by the reaction – and not by simple mixture – of its oxidising and combustible constituents.

In short, whatever the explosive consists of, with such power – more than enough to toss a projectile weighing 80,000 tonnes beyond the pull of gravity – it is clear that the recoil it will pass back to the cannon will produce the following effects: a shift of axis; displacement of the pole by 23°28'; perpendicularity of the new axis to the plane of the ecliptic. Thence all the disasters so rightly feared by the Earth's inhabitants will occur.

However, there remains one chance for humanity to escape the consequences of an operation that will so transform our planet's geographical and climatological conditions.

Is it really possible to build a cannon of such dimensions that it would have a million times the volume of the 27cm cannon? Whatever the progress of our metallurgy industry – building the Tay and Forth bridges, Garabit viaducts, Eiffel towers and the like – is it conceivable that engineers will be able to produce this gigantic machine, not to mention the 180,000-tonne projectile it would launch into space?

We may permit ourselves a degree of doubt. Clearly, this is one reason among the many for the possible failure of Barbicane & Co.'s attempt. Yet it leaves open a number of particularly worrying possibilities, since it seems that the society has already moved into action.

As we well know, Barbicane and Nicholl have left Baltimore and America altogether. They have been gone more than two months. Where are they? Most certainly in that unknown corner of the planet where all is to be set up for their operation.

Now, where is this place? We do not know and, consequently, it is impossible for us to pursue these foolhardy 'gangsters', who are threatening to turn the world upside down under the pretext of developing newly accessible coal mines for their private profit.

Of course, it is now apparent that this place must have been named in J-T Maston's notebook, on the last page, where he summarized his conclusions. However, that last page was shredded by the teeth of that associate of Impey

Barbicane, and Maston, now incarcerated in Baltimore prison, absolutely refuses to talk.

Such, then, is our position. If President Barbicane succeeds in building his monstrous cannon and projectile; in short, if his project is carried out in the manner detailed above, he will alter the old axis and in six months the Earth will be subject to this 'unpardonable experiment'.

Indeed, a date has been chosen for the firing to unleash its entire, untrammelled force; on that date the impact transferred to our ellipsoid Earth will attain maximum intensity.

That date is 22nd September, twelve hours after the Sun's passage over the meridian of the place 'x'.

So we know the following facts: (1) That the firing will be carried out by a cannon one million times larger than the 27cm cannon; (2) That the cannon will be loaded with a projectile weighing 180,000 tonnes; (3) That this projectile will be fired at an initial speed of 1,800km per second; (4) That the shot will be fired on 22nd September, twelve hours after the Sun's passage over the meridian of the place. Can we therefore deduce from these circumstances where place x must be?

In fact, we cannot, since nothing in J-T Maston's workings suggests in what direction the new axis will shift; in other words, nothing tells us where the Earth's new poles will be located. At 23°28' from the former poles, of course. But on what meridian – that remains entirely impossible to ascertain.

It is, therefore, impossible for us to know which lands will be lowered and which raised, following change in sea-levels, nor which continents will be turned into oceans and which oceans transformed into continents.

Yet this change in levels will be quite considerable, according to J-T Maston's calculations. After the impact, the surface of the seas will take a new ellipsoid shape, according to the planet's revolution around a new polar axis, and water levels will be altered at almost every point on the planet.

'The intersection of the new and former sea levels,' writes J-T Maston in his notebook, '– two equal surfaces in rotation whose axes meet – will be made up of two flat curves, both of whose planes will pass at a perpendicular angle to the plane of the two polar axes, and respectively to the two bisectors of the angle of each of the two polar axes.'

It follows from this that the maximum achievable change in sea levels would be an elevation or lowering of 8,415m compared to former levels, and on some parts of the planet, certain territories will be lowered or raised by as much as this. This degree of change will diminish gradually in the direction of the demarcating borderlines, which divide the planet into four segments and along which the change in level will be nil.

It is also worth noting that the former pole should itself be submerged under more than 3,000m of water, once it is relocated to a position nearer the Earth's centre, due to the flattening of our sphere. This means that the land acquired by the North Polar Exploitation Association should be flooded and thereby rendered inaccessible. But this eventuality has been anticipated by Barbicane & Co and geographical considerations deduced from their latest discoveries give them reason to believe in the existence of an Arctic plateau currently situated at more than 3,000m above sea level.

As for those places on Earth where the re-levelling is set to reach 8,415m, which will consequently undergo the worst of its consequences, no one can claim to determine what will happen there. The most ingenious of calculators would not manage it. There is in this equation an unknown which no formula can reveal. This is precisely the problem of location x from where the shot is to be fired, and, thence, the location of the impact... Thus, this x is the heart of the secret guarded by the pursuers of this deplorable affair.

So, to conclude, no matter which latitude they live in, the Earth's inhabitants have a direct interest in knowing this secret, since they are directly threatened by the actions of Barbicane & Co.

Consequently, inhabitants of Europe, Africa, Asia, America, Australasia and Oceania are advised to look out for all new works of a ballistic nature, such as smelting of armaments, or manufacture of gunpowder or of missiles, that might be undertaken in their part of the world, and to be vigilant with regard to any strangers whose presence might appear suspicious, and straight away to inform the members of the Commission of Inquiry in Baltimore, Maryland, USA.

May the Heavens grant that this disclosure come before the 22nd September of this year, which date is threatening to throw the entire established order of our planet's functioning into turmoil.

XII

IN WHICH J-T MASTON PERSISTS
IN HIS HEROIC SILENCE

So, following the cannon to launch a projectile from the Earth
to the Moon, the world now has a cannon to alter the Earth's
axis. Cannon; always cannon. But these Gun Club artillery-
men have nothing else in their heads. They are caught up in
a craze for 'extreme cannonisation'. They see the cannon as
the final answer to everything in this world. Just as canon law
governs theology, can the mighty cannon also have the final
word in the courts of commerce and the cosmos?

In fact, it was natural that President Barbicane and his
colleagues should straight away think of that machine, the
cannon. You cannot devote your life to ballistics and not expect
a few negative consequences. After building the *Columbiad*
in Florida*, they were bound to go on to the monster cannon
of…, that is, of the unknown place *x*. You can imagine them
crying out in ringing voices:

'Aim for the Moon! First cannon… Fire!'

'Shift the Earth's axis! Second cannon… Fire!'

In the meanwhile, the command the whole world ached
to call:

'To hell! Third cannon… Fire!'

And really, their project quite justified the title of this book,
The Earth Turned Upside Down, for soon there would no
longer be any 'up' or 'down' and, as Alcide Pierdeux put it,
this would be followed by 'a worldwide upheaval'.

---

* [Giant cannon conceived in Verne's *From the Earth to the Moon*, the novel that
preceded *The Earth Turned Upside Down*.]

Be that as it may, the publication of the communiqué drafted by the Commission of Enquiry produced incalculable uproar. But then it had hardly been intended to reassure. With J-T Maston's calculations, it seemed that the mechanical challenge had been resolved down to the smallest detail. The operation itself, to be carried out by President Barbicane and Captain Nicholl – this part was only too clear – would cause a highly regrettable alteration in the diurnal rotation. A brand-new axis would replace the old one… And we know what the consequences of this change would be.

The project of Barbicane & Co. was thus judged, cursed and denounced, amidst the general disapproval. On the old as well as on the new continent, the North Polar Exploitation Association's board-members found nothing but enemies. If any supporters remained among the wild cards of America, they were rare.

From the point of view of their personal security, President Barbicane and Captain Nicholl had been wise to leave Baltimore and America. There was reason to believe they would have come to some misfortune. You cannot threaten 1,400 million people, sow havoc in their lives by changing the living conditions on Earth, make them fear for their very existences by provoking worldwide disaster – and expect to get off scot-free

But how had those two Gun Club leaders managed to disappear without a trace? How could they have transported the materials and assistance required for such an operation without anyone seeing them? Hundreds of carriages, if they had gone by train, or hundreds of ships, if it were by sea, would not have sufficed to carry the cargos of metal, coal and dyna-mix. It was thoroughly mystifying that this departure could have been made incognito. And yet it had. Besides, following a comprehensive inquiry, it was established that no orders had been sent to either the metallurgical or the chemical factories in either of the two continents. The thing was inexplicable. But never mind. It would be explained in years to come... if there were any years left to come.

All the same, while the mysteriously vanished President Barbicane and Captain Nicholl were safe from immediate danger, their colleague J-T Maston, duly secured under lock and key, might have everything to fear from public reprisals. But he was not the least concerned. How admirably stubborn our mathematician was. A will of iron, just like his forearm. Nothing could make him yield.

Ensconced in his cell in the Baltimore prison, the Gun Club secretary's thoughts turned increasingly to wondering about those far-away colleagues he had been unable to follow. He tried to picture President Barbicane and Captain Nicholl preparing their vast operation in that unknown corner of the world where no one would bother them. He could see them building their enormous machine, combining their dyna-mix, smelting the projectile that the Sun might soon count among her daintier planets. This brand-new heavenly body would bear the charming name Scorbetta, a mark of gallantry and esteem for the wealthy capitaliste of New Park. And J-T Maston was counting down the days – and they did seem to fly by – each of which brought nearer the date fixed for firing the cannon.

It was already early April. In two and a half months, after pausing over the tropic of Cancer at the solstice, the sun would retreat towards the tropic of Capricorn. Three months later, it would cross the equator on the autumn equinox. And then, all would be over for these seasons that, for millions of centuries, had alternated so regularly – and stupidly – throughout each year on Earth. The year 1891 would be the last to subject the

Earth to inequalities between days and nights. Thereafter we should have only equal numbers of hours between the Sun's rising and its setting over any horizon on the planet.

In fact, this would be a stupendous achievement, super-human, godlike. Forgetting the arctic region and the development of coal mines beneath the former pole, J-T Maston gazed only upon the cosmographic consequences of their project. The new society's primary aim was dwarfed by these transformations that would change the face of the world.

This, of course, neglected the fact that the world did not want its face changed. Was it not forever young, the face that God had given it in the first hours of creation?

As for J-T Maston, alone and vulnerable in his cell, he kept up his resistance to every pressure brought to bear on him. Members of the Commission of Inquiry came to visit daily, but made no headway. It was then that John H. Prestice had the idea of harnessing an influence that might be greater than theirs: that of Mrs Evangelina Scorbitt. All were aware of that respectable widow's devotion when it came to J-T Maston and of the limitless interest she took in the famous mathematician.

So, following consultation with the commissioners, Mrs Evangelina Scorbitt was authorized to go and see the prisoner as often as she wished. After all, she was in as much danger from the monster cannon's recoil as the rest of the Earth's inhabitants. Her New Park mansion would not be spared the final catastrophe any more than the humblest fur-trapper's hut or Prairie Indian's wigwam. Her future existence was as much in doubt as that of the last of the Samoyeds or the obscurest islander in the Pacific. This is what the ppresident of the commission gave her to understand; this is why they begged her to use her influence on J-T Maston.

Were the latter to decide at last to talk, should he choose to reveal where President Barbicane and Captain Nicholl – and doubtless a multitude of assistants whom they must have added to their party – were busy with their preparations, there might still be time to go looking for them, to pick up their tracks, to put an end to the torments, agonies and terrors of humanity.

Thus Mrs Evangelina Scorbitt was given access to the prison. What she wanted above all was to see J-T Maston once more, rescued from the hands of the police and happily back in his cottage.

But to think that the energetic Evangelina would be slave to such human weakness was seriously to misjudge her. If, on 9th April, the first time Mrs Evangelina Scorbitt closed the door to Maston's cell behind her, some indiscreet ear were to be glued to it, this is what that ear would have heard – with some surprise, perhaps:

'At last, dear Maston, I see you once more!'

'You? Mrs Scorbitt?'

'Yes, dear friend, after four weeks, four long weeks of separation…'

'Exactly twenty-eight days, five hours and forty-five minutes,' replied J-T Maston, on consulting his watch.

'At last we are reunited!'

'But how have you been able to reach me, dear Mrs Scorbitt?'

'On condition that I use all the influence I possess as a result of my boundless affection for he who stands in front of me!'

'What! Evangelina!' gasped J-T Maston. 'You would consent to give me such advice! … You really imagine I could ever betray our colleagues?'

'I? Dear Maston! ... Do you then think so little of me? ... I, beg you to sacrifice your honour for mere safety? ... I, impel you to an act that would cover in shame a life wholly devoted to the highest calculations in transcendental mechanics!'

'Very good, Mrs Scorbitt! I do indeed once more see in you our society's most generous patron! No... I never doubted the stoutness of your heart!'

'Thank you, dear Maston.'

'As for me, to divulge our work; to disclose where in the world our prodigious shot shall be fired; to sell, as it were, the secret I was so happily able to hide deep inside me; to allow those barbarians to set off in pursuit of our friends; to break off the work that will be our fortune and our glory... I would rather die!'

'Sublime Maston!' breathed Evangelina Scorbitt.

In truth, these two creatures, so closely united by the same passion – and each as mad as the other, what's more – understood each other perfectly.

'No! They shall never know the name of the country designated by my calculations and whose fame shall be immortal!' added J-T Maston. 'They can kill me, if they wish, but they will never tear my secret from me!'

'Let them kill me too!' cried Mrs Evangelina Scorbitt. 'I too, I shall be mute...'

'Luckily, dear Evangelina, they do not know that you share our secret.'

Do you then think, dear Maston, that I should be capable of revealing it, because I am merely a woman? And betray our colleagues and you! ... No, my friend, no! Let these philistines raise the populations of the towns and the countryside against you; let the whole world come in by this cell door to tear you away, what of it? I shall be there, and we shall at least have the consolation of dying together…'

As if there could be any greater consolation for J-T Maston than that of dying in the arms of Mrs Evangelina Scorbitt.

That is how the conversation ended on every occasion the excellent lady went to visit the prisoner.

And when the commissioners questioned her on the results of her discussions:

'Nothing yet!' She would say. 'Perhaps with time I shall get there…'

'With time', she would say. But time was marching on by great strides. The weeks flew by like days, the days like hours and the hours like minutes.

It was already May. It seemed that Mrs Evangelina Scorbitt had found out nothing from J-T Maston, and where such an influential lady had failed, no other had any hope of success. Must everyone now resign themselves to waiting for the terrible event, without a chance of stopping it?

But no. In such circumstances, resignation is unacceptable. In fact, the European powers' delegates became more determined than ever. There was constant conflict between them and the members of the Commission of Inquiry, whom they did not hesitate to take to task. Even the phlegmatic Jacques Jansen, despite his Dutch placidity, could be seen daily pouring abuse on the commissioners. Colonel Boris Karkof even fought a duel with the secretary of the commission – although his adversary got away with only a scratch. As for Major Donellan, while he fought neither with firearms nor with knives – which are, besides, contrary to British custom – he did at least, abetted by his secretary Dean Toodrink, exchange a few dozen blows in an all-out boxing match with William S. Forster, the poker-faced codfish dealer, the North

Polar Exploitation Association's straw man, who, moreover, knew nothing at all about the business.

In fact the entire world was conspiring to find the United States responsible for the acts of one of her most brilliant offspring, Impey Barbicane. There was talk of nothing less than withdrawing the ambassadors and ministerial envoys assigned to this wayward government in Washington, and of declaring war on it.

Poor United States! She wanted nothing more than to track down Barbicane & Co. In vain did she announce that the great powers of Europe, Asia, Africa and Oceania were authorized to arrest the men anywhere they might be found; nobody even listened. And still, it proved impossible to find out where the president and his colleague were making their abominable preparations.

To which the foreign powers replied: 'You have their accomplice, J-T Maston! Now, J-T Maston has the ear and confidence of Barbicane. So: make J-T Maston talk.'

Make J-T Maston talk! You might as well try to drag a word from the mouth of Harpocrate, god of silence, or from the head deaf-mute at the New York Institute.

At this stage, their exasperation growing along with the general anxiety, some practical types recalled that there was much to be said for mediaeval torture: the sworn-in master torturer's boots; the nipple tongs; molten lead, sovereign for loosening the most mutinous tongues; boiling oil; the rack; waterboarding, strappado; etc. Why not make use of these resources that the law had not hesitated to employ previously in circumstances infinitely less serious or for special cases that hardly affected the mass of people?

Still, it must be admitted: those methods justified by earlier moral codes could no longer be applied at the end of a century of gentleness and tolerance, of a century as imbued with humaneness as this nineteenth after Christ, marked by the invention of the repeating rifle and of seven-millimetre bullets capable of shooting under unbelievable pressures; of a century that sanctions the use of melinite, roburite, bellite, panclastite and meganite shells, and many other substances ending in –ite, which are nothing, it is true, compared to our dyna-mix.

J-T Maston had, therefore, nothing to fear from being subjected to questioning, ordinary or extraordinary. All that might be hoped was that, at last appreciating his responsibility, he might perhaps decide to talk, or, if he continued to refuse, that luck might do the talking for him.

XIII

AT THE END OF WHICH J-T MASTON
MAKES A TRULY EPIC REPLY

Time was marching on; however so too, in all likelihood, were President Barbicane and Captain Nicholl, making the preparations for their Earth-shattering project in a place that was entirely unknown to the rest of the world.

Yet, how was it that an operation that called for the erection of a substantial production plant, the construction of great furnaces capable of casting a machine a million times bigger than the navy's 27cm cannon and a projectile weighing 180,000 tonnes, which would require the hiring of several thousand labourers, their transport, their facilities, etc; how was it that such an operation could be concealed from such keenly interested parties? In what corner of the Old or New Continents might Barbicane & Co. secretly have installed themselves yet never roused suspicion among the local people? Was it on a deserted island in the Pacific or the Indian Ocean? But there are no desert islands left these days: the English have nabbed them all. Unless the new society had discovered one for this purpose? As for the idea that the factories might have been set up somewhere in the Arctic or Antarctic regions – no, that would have been quite absurd. Was it not precisely due to the inaccessibility of these extreme latitudes that the North Polar Exploitation Association was trying to reposition them?

Besides, searching for President Barbicane and Captain Nicholl through these continents and islands would have been a waste of time. The notebook seized at the Gun Club secretary's house mentioned that the shot would be fired more or less from the equator. Now, there *are* habitable regions there, even if none of them is inhabited by civilized men. If the experimenters had established their base somewhere along the line of the equinox, it could be neither in America, nor anywhere within the expanses of Peru or Brazil, nor in the Sonde Islands, Sumatra or Borneo, nor in the islands in the Celebes Sea, nor in New Guinea, where such operations could not be conducted without the populations' knowledge. Very probably, too, it could not have been kept secret anywhere in central Africa, in the region of the great lakes, where they lie across the equator. That left the Maldives in the Indian Ocean, the Admiralty, Gilbert, Christmas and Galapagos Islands in the Pacific, and San Pedro in the Atlantic. But requests for information drew a blank in all of these various locations. So the searchers were reduced to vague conjectures, ill-suited to calming severe worldwide jitters.

And what was Alcide Pierdeux's opinion of all this? More 'Sulphuric Alcide' than ever, he could not stop pondering the various consequences of the problem. That Captain Nicholl should have invented such a powerful explosive, that he should have discovered this dyna-mix, whose force was three or four times greater than that of the most powerful explosives currently used in battle, and 5,600 times more powerful than the good old gunpowder our ancestors used; already this was quite electrifying – 'even highly sense-defying!' he thought to himself – yet everything considered, it was not impossible. We can never know what the future has in store for us when it comes to this kind of progress, enabling armies to be wiped out from whatever distance we like. In any case, the alteration of the Earth's axis produced by recoil from a gunshot was not about to surprise our French engineer. Then, addressing himself as if confidentially to the promoter of the whole business, he muttered:

'It is quite clear, President Barbicane, that the Earth absorbs the repercussions of all the blows caused to its surface, every day. We know that when hundreds of thousands of men play at sending thousands of missiles each weighing a few kilos at each other, or millions of missiles weighing a few grammes each, or even, simply, when I walk or jump or stretch out my arm, or when a blood cell floats along my veins, that has an effect on our planet's mass. Evidently your great invention is capable of producing the necessary jolt. But, holy hypotenuse! Will that jolt be enough to knock the Earth sideways? Well, that is what the equations of that devil J-T Maston irrefutably demonstrate, you have to admit!'

Indeed, Alcide Pierdeux could not help but admire the Gun Club Secretary's ingenious calculations, as conveyed by the Commission of Inquiry's members to those scholars in a position to understand them. And Alcide Pierdeux, who perused algebra as you and I read the morning papers, found it made inexpressibly delightful reading.

But if the sideways knock did happen, what disasters would be sparked along the Earth's surface! What cataclysms, cities overturned, mountains undermined, people killed in their millions, bodies of water shot out of their basins and causing horrific damage!

It would be like an incomparably violent earthquake.

'If only,' muttered Alcide Pierdeux, 'if only Captain Nicholl's blasted gunpowder were not so powerful, we could pray that, having gone once round the planet, the projectile would fall back and strike the Earth, either just short of the spot where the shot was fired, or just beyond it. Then, everything would drop back into place relatively quickly – not without having caused some terrible disasters in the meantime. But to hell with it! Thanks to their dyna-mix, the cannonball will give a half-curve of a hyperbola and never once return to beg the Earth's pardon for bothering her, by knocking her back into place!'

And, gesticulating like a semaphore tower, Alcide Pierdeux only just avoided smashing everything within a two-metre radius.

Then, he repeated to himself: 'If only we knew the site of the cannon, I would soon be able to work out which broad areas will be unaffected by the re-levelling and likewise the places that will be most seriously affected. We would be able to warn people to leave home in time, before their houses and towns all come down on their noggins. But how to find it out?'

Upon which, absently smoothing down the few hairs that still decorated his skull, Pierdeux added: 'Ah! Now I'm thinking: the consequences of the jolt might be more complicated than we imagine. Why should the volcanoes not take advantage of the occasion to embark on a frenzy of eruptions; like a seasick passenger, to start vomiting all the elements redirected into their bellies? Why should a mass of upraised ocean not be dashed into their craters? The Devil take us all! Such explosions could blow out the whole terrestrial system! Oh, that demon Maston, so determined in his silence! Can't you just picture him, tossing our ball about, proudly finessing his shots in his great billiards game in the sky!'

Thus reasoned Alcide Pierdeux. Soon these alarming hypotheses would be taken up and discussed by newspapers across the two continents. Next to the upheaval that would result from Barbicane & Co.'s operations, why fuss about those whirlwinds, tidal waves and floods that now and then might devastate some small, discrete portion of the Earth? Such misfortunes are but partial. A few thousand people are lost, hardly troubling the tranquillity of the innumerable survivors.

So it was that as the fatal date drew nearer, even the bravest succumbed to terror. It was only too easy for preachers to predict the world's imminent end now. You might have imagined the world gone back to that terrifying moment in the year 1000 when the living believed they were about to be dashed down into the realm of the dead.

Let's recall what happened then. Upon reading a certain passage in the Book of Revelation, the populations came to believe that the day of last judgment was near. They watched for signs of anger, as forecast by the Scripture. The son of perdition, the Antichrist, was going to be revealed.

'In the last year of the tenth century,' H. Martin recounts, 'everything was interrupted: games, business, interests, everything; even those working the land thought of stopping. Why, people said, why look to a future that will not happen? Let us think on the eternity that will begin tomorrow! Only the most immediate requirements were looked after; lands and castles were bequeathed to the monasteries, to guarantee protectors in the kingdom of heaven, where everyone was destined so soon. Many contemporary charters recording donations to churches begin with the words: "The end of the world being near and her destruction imminent…" When the fatal date arrived, people crowded endlessly into the basilicas, the chapels and all consecrated edifices, and waited, in agonies of terror, for the seven trumpets of the seven angels of judgment to ring out from high in the sky.'

As we know, the first day of the year 1000 came to an end without nature's laws experiencing the least disruption. But this time round, it was not a case of hysteria inspired by texts of biblical obscurity. It was a question of modification to the Earth's equilibrium, based on rock-solid, unarguable calculations, and of an experiment that the progress of the ballistic and mechanical sciences rendered entirely possible. This time it should not be the dead rising out of the sea, but the living sucked down by their millions, to the depths of her brand-new abysses.

It followed that, even considering psychological changes wrought by the influence of modern ideas, the general terror now reached such a point that a number of practices adopted in 1000 were taken up again, in response to the same impulse of panic. Never had preparations for departure to a better world been made in such a hurry! Never had cascades of sins been so abundantly spouted inside the confessionals! Never had so many absolutions been granted to those dying and repenting *in extremis*! There was even talk of asking for a general absolution, by means of papal brief applying to all men of good will upon the Earth – and there was also, simply, full-blown terror.

In these circumstances, J-T Maston's situation was growing more critical every day. Mrs Evangelina Scorbitt trembled to think of his falling victim to worldwide condemnation. She may even have considered advising him to pronounce the words that he, in his unparalleled obstinacy, was determined not to speak. But, luckily, she did not dare. That would have gained nothing but a categoric refusal.

As you may well imagine, even in the town of Baltimore, now also prey to the terror, it was becoming difficult to contain the population, whipped up by all the newspapers of America and by the dispatches arriving from 'all four corners of the Earth', to borrow the apocalyptic language favoured by St John the Evangelist in the times of Domitian. Without a doubt, had J-T Maston lived in the reign of that despot, his case would swiftly have been solved. He would have been fed to wild beasts. Although he would simply have replied:

'I'm there already!'

Be that as it may, the unshakeable J-T Maston still refused to reveal the location of place x, knowing quite well that if he did reveal it, President Barbicane and Captain Nicholl would find themselves unable to pursue their project.

It was sublime, after all, this struggle of a single man against the whole world. This raised J-T Maston even further in Mrs Evangelina Scorbitt's estimation and also in the opinion of his Gun Club colleagues. These brave gentlemen, it should be said, as headstrong as any retired artillery-men, continued to root for Barbicane & Co.'s projects. The Gun Club's Secretary had reached such a degree of celebrity that many were already writing to him, as happens with distinguished criminals, in order to receive a few lines from the hand that was about to turn the world upside down.

Yet, while sublime, things were also growing more and more dangerous. The masses clustered day and night around the prison in Baltimore, surrounding J-T Maston with great shouts and tumult. The furious people wanted to lynch him here and now. The police could imagine that they might soon be powerless to defend him.

Wishing to bring some satisfaction to the American populace as well as to people of other nations, the government in Washington at last decided to indict J-T Maston and bring him before the courts.

Brought before these jurors, who were as gripped as any by the frenzy of terror, 'his case would not take long!' as Alcide Pierdeux commented; though for his part he felt a certain sympathy for the mathematician's dogged nature.

The next step was for the president of the Commission of Inquiry to go in person to see the prisoner in his cell. It was the morning of 5th September.

Upon her earnest request, Mrs Evangelina Scorbitt was authorized to accompany him. Perhaps, with one last attempt, the influence of this enchanting lady might just win the day? … No possibility must be neglected. All means were permitted, if they stood a chance of revealing the key to the mystery. And if this attempt were unsuccessful? Well, then we should see.

'Indeed we shall see!' echoed shrewd heads. 'That'll make all the difference: if we hang J-T Maston and disaster strikes anyway, in all its horror!'

So, at about eleven o'clock, J-T Maston found himself in the presence of Mrs Evangelina Scorbitt and John H. Prestice, president of the Commission of Inquiry.

The preliminaries were simple. The following questions and replies were exchanged in dialogue, very tense on the one side, very calm on the other, (and who would have believed that the day would come when J-T Maston would be the calm one?)

'For the last time, will you answer!' asked John H. Prestice.

'To what question?' responded the Gun Club Secretary wryly.

'To the question of where your colleague Barbicane has vanished to.'

'I have already told you a hundred times.'

'Repeat it for the hundred and first.'

'He is where the shot will be fired.'

'And where will the shot be fired?'

'Where my colleague Barbicane is.'

'Look out for yourself, J-T Maston!'

'For what?'

'For the consequences of your refusal to reply, which will…'

'Which will, as intended, stop you from learning what you ought not to know.'

'What we have a right to know!'

'That is not my opinion.'

'We shall call you before the courts!'

'Call away.'

'And the jury will find you guilty!'

'That's their business.'

'And the sentence: no sooner passed than it shall be executed!'

'So be it!'

'Dear Maston! …' Mrs Evangelina Scorbitt dared to pronounce, her heart troubled by these threats.

'Oh! … Mrs Scorbitt!' exclaimed J-T Maston.

She lowered her head and said nothing.

'And would you like to know what the sentence will be?' continued Commission President John H. Prestice.

'As you will,' J-T Maston replied.

'It is that you will be condemned to death… as you deserve!'

'Really?'

'And you will be hanged, as surely as two plus two makes four.'

'Then, Sir, I still have a chance,' J-T Maston replied calmly. 'If you knew anything of mathematics, you would not say "as surely as two plus two makes four"! What proof have you that all the mathematicians up to now have not been fools to assert that the sum of two numbers is equal to that of their parts, which is to say that two and two makes exactly four?'

'Sir!' gasped the President, absolutely lost for words.

'Now,' J-T Maston went on, 'if you were to say "as surely as one plus one makes two", that would be fine! That is absolutely obvious, for it is no longer a theory but a definition!'

Upon which arithmetic lesson, the president of the ommission withdrew, while Mrs Evangelina Scorbitt could not instil her gaze with sufficient fire to match her admiration for the extraordinary mathematician of her dreams!

XIV

VERY BRIEF, BUT IN WHICH PLACE 'X' GAINS A GEOGRAPHICAL VALUE

Fortunately for J-T Maston, the American government then received the following telegram, sent by the American consul in Zanzibar:

> *To John S Wright, Minister of State,*
> *Washington, USA.*
>
> *Zanzibar, 13th September*
>
> *5 o'clock in the morning, local time*
>
> *Large-scale works undertaken in the Wamasai, to the South of Kilimanjaro craters. For the last eight months, Impey Barbicane and Captain Nicholl, installed with many black assistants, under the authority of Sultan Bali-Bali. This brought to the attention of the government by your devoted*
> > *RICHARD W TRUST, consul*

And that is how J-T Maston's secret came out. And that is why, although the Gun Club Secretary was kept in a state of incarceration, he was not hanged.

Who knows, however, if later on he might feel a belated regret, not having died at the height of his glory…

XV

WHICH CONTAINS SOME GENUINELY INTERESTING DETAILS FOR THE EARTH'S INHABITANTS

So it was that Washington now knew where Barbicane & Co. were carrying out their operation. The authenticity of the dispatch was undeniable. The consul of Zanzibar was entirely dependable and his information required no further corroboration. It was confirmed to the letter by subsequent telegrams. And it was indeed in the centre of the Kilimanjaro region, in the African Wamasai, about a hundred leagues west of the coast, a little below the equator, that the North Polar Exploitation Association's engineers were on the verge of completing their prodigious task.

How had they been able to establish themselves secretly in this forgotten land, at the foot of the famous mountain, reconnoitred in 1849 by Doctors Rebviani and Krapf, and subsequently scaled by the travellers Otto Ehlers and Abbot? How had they managed to set up their workshops, build a foundry, gather sufficient assistance there? By what means had they succeeded in treating with the country's hostile tribes and their leaders, no less cunning than they were cruel? That remained unknown. And perhaps we should never know it, for there were only a few days to go before the 22nd September.

So, when J-T Maston learned from Mrs Evangelina Scorbitt that the mystery of Kilimanjaro had just been revealed by a dispatch sent from Zanzibar, he was sanguine:

'Pah!' he said, cutting an extravagant zigzag in the air with his iron hook. 'We cannot yet travel by telegraph or by telephone, and in six days… patarapatanboomboom! It'll be in the bag!'

And whoever happened to hear the secretary of the Gun Club let fly that resounding onomatopoeia, which rang out like a shot from the *Columbiad*, would have been truly amazed at how much vital energy remains in these old artillery-men.

Plainly J-T Maston was right. There was not enough time to send agents as far as the Wamasai to arrest President Barbicane. Even allowing for the possibility that agents leaving from Algeria or Egypt, even from Aden, Massouah, Madagascar or Zanzibar, might rapidly have arrived at the coast, they would still have had to contend with the particular difficulties of that land: delays caused by obstacles to advancing through that mountainous region, and also perhaps by the reluctance of a staff sustained, no doubt, by the self-interest of a sultan as authoritarian as he was black.

It seemed then that there was no longer any hope of preventing the operation by arresting the operators.

Nevertheless, while arrest was impossible, nothing could now be easier than to work out the precise consequences of the shot, since its exact position was now known. It was a matter of pure calculation – rather complex calculation, naturally, but not beyond the skills of algebraists in particular and mathematicians in general.

Since the consul's dispatch had been addressed directly to the Minister of State in Washington, the American government had at first kept it secret. It was hoping also to be able to indicate – upon revealing the news – what the effect of displacing the Earth's axis would be on sea levels around the world. The Earth's inhabitants – desperate to find out where they stood, and where they would stand in future – would then also learn what fate awaited them, on the particular portion of the Earth's surface they occupied.

On 14th September, the dispatch was sent to the Bureau for Longitudes in Washington, which was charged with working out the ultimate consequences, from both ballistic and geographical points of view. By the following day, the situation was clearly established. The Old World was notified of the results by cable and the New World by telegram. After news of the predicted consequences had been published by thousands of newspapers, it was the sole topic of conversation in the great cities and elsewhere.

'What will happen?' This was the question being asked in every language in every place on the planet.

And this is the reply that was offered with the approval of the Bureau for Longitudes.

URGENT NOTICE

The experiment being attempted by President Barbicane and Captain Nicholl is as follows: on 22nd September, at midnight local time, to produce a recoil by means of a cannon a million times bigger than the 27cm cannon, launching of a 180,000-tonne projectile with cannon powder, leading to an initial speed of 2,800km.

If this shot is effected at a little below the equinoctial line, almost at longitude 34° east of the Paris meridian, from the base of the Kilimanjaro highlands, and if it is directed southwards, the following effects will be caused to the planet's surface as a result:

Instantaneously, due to the combination of the impact with the usual diurnal movement, a new axis will be created and, since the former axis will, according to J-T Maston's figures, be displaced by 23°28', the new axis will be per-pendicular to the ecliptic plane.

Where now will the two new poles be located? The location of the shot now being known, it has become simple to work this out.

The northern end of the new axis will be located between Greenland and Grinnell Land, in that part of the Baffin Sea that currently lies over the Arctic Polar Circle. The southern end will be on the edge of the current Antarctic Polar Circle, a few degrees east of Adélie Land.

In these circumstances, starting at the new North Pole, a new zero meridian will run approximately through Dublin in Ireland, Paris in France, Palermo in Sicily, the Gulf of Great Syrtis on the coast of Tripoli, El Obeid in Darfur, the highlands of Kilimanjaro, Madagascar, the Kerguelen Islands in the Southern Pacific, the new South Pole, the antipodes of Paris, the Cook and Society Islands in Oceania, the Quadra and Vancouver Islands off the coast of British Columbia, through North America via the territory of New Britain and the Melville Peninsula, to end in the North Polar regions.

Following the creation of this new rotational axis with its extremes located in the Baffin Sea to the north and in Adélie Land to the south, there will be a new equator, along which the Sun will follow its diurnal path without deviation. This equinoctial line will go through Kilimanjaro at Wamasai, through the Indian Ocean, Goa and Chicacole in India, just skimming below Calcutta, through Mangala in the Kingdom of Siam, Kesho in the Tonkin, Hong Kong in China, Rasa Island, the Marshall Islands, Gaspar-Rico, Walker Island in the Pacific, the Cordillera of the Republic of Argentina, Rio de Janeiro in Brazil, the Trinity Islands and Saint Helena in the Atlantic, Saint Paul de Loanda in the Congo, before rejoining the lands of Wamasai and the far side of Kilimanjaro.

This new Equator being thus determined by the creation of the new axis, it has become possible to analyse the problem of changes in sea-level, which is so urgent for the safety of the Earth's inhabitants.

First and foremost, it should be noted that the North Polar Exploitation Association's officials are taking every pre-caution to attenuate these effects as far as possible. Indeed, were the shot to be fired towards the north, the consequences would be disastrous for the Earth's most civilized regions. On the contrary, by aiming to the south, these consequences will be felt only among wild and less populated regions – at least as regards those areas facing submersion.

The following describes how the seas will be re-distributed, once forced out of their basins by the planet's flattening at the sites of the former poles.

The planet can be seen as divided into two great circles, intersecting at right angles at Kilimanjaro and at its antipode in the equatorial ocean. Thence, we can divide it further, into four sections: two in the northern hemisphere and two in the southern, each separated by lines along which there will be zero re-levelling.

1. The northern hemisphere:
   The first section, to the west of Kilimanjaro, will include Africa from the Congo up to Egypt, Europe from Turkey to Greenland, America from British Columbia as far as Peru and into Brazil as far as Salvador – in short, it includes the whole of the North Atlantic Ocean and the majority of the equatorial Atlantic.

The second section, to the east of Kilimanjaro, will include the majority of Europe from the Black Sea up to Sweden, both European and Asian parts of Russia, Arabia, almost the whole of India, Persia, Baluchistan, Afghanistan, Turkestan, the Celestial Empire, Mongolia, Japan, Korea, the Black Sea, the Caspian Sea, the northern end of the Pacific and the North American territories of Alaska – as well as the polar region so unfortunately ceded to the American society of the North Polar Exploitation Association.

2. The southern hemisphere:

The third section, to the east of Kilimanjaro, will include Madagascar, the Prince Edward Islands, the Kerguelen Islands, Mauritius, Réunion and all the islands of the Indian Ocean, the Antarctic Ocean as far as the new pole, the peninsula of Malacca, Java, Sumatra, Borneo, the Sonde Islands, the Philippines, Australia, New Zealand, New Guinea, New Caledonia, and the whole southern end of the Pacific, with all its many archipelagos, about as far as the today's longitude 160°.

The fourth section, to the west of Kilimanjaro, will take in the southern part of Africa, from the Congo and the Mozambique Channel as far as the Cape of Good Hope, the South Atlantic Ocean down to latitude 80°, the whole of South America from Pernambuco, through Lima, Bolivia, Brazil, Uruguay, the Argentine Republic, Patagonia, Terra del Fuego, the Falkland Islands, Sandwich, Shetland and the South Pacific as far east as longitude 160°.

This describes our four sections of the planet, their borders forming linear regions of zero re-levelling.

We now outline the effects to be expected at the surface of each section following displacement of the seas.

In each section, there is a central point where the maximum effect will be sustained, whether that be flooding or drought.

Now, the perfect precision of J-T Maston's calculations have established that the maximum raising or lowering experienced will be 8,415m at each central point, from where the degree of re-levelling will diminish until the neutral lines forming the sectional borders are reached. It is therefore at the central points that the effects will be most serious from the point of view of general safety, due to President Barbicane's operation.

Every possible consequence of both raising and lowering should be considered.

In two of the four sections, located diagonally opposite each other, one in the Northern hemisphere, one in the southern, the seas will draw back – in order to rush into the other two sections, likewise located in diagonal opposition in each hemisphere.

In the first section: the Atlantic Ocean will be almost completely drained and, its lowest point being about where Bermuda lies, if the sea's depth at that point is less than 8,415m, the seabed will be uncovered. Consequently, a series of substantial territories will appear between Europe and America, that the United States, England, France, Spain or Portugal may annex, depending on their respective geographic extent, should these great powers choose. But we must observe that following the drop in sea level, the layer of atmospheric air will also drop, accordingly. The coasts of Europe and America will thus effectively be raised so that even towns positioned twenty or thirty degrees away from the central points shall find at their disposal no more than the quantity of air currently measured at a height of one league. So (to name only the principal among them): New York, Philadelphia, Charleston, Panama, Lisbon, Madrid, Paris, London, Edinburgh, Dublin, etc. Only Cairo, Constantinople, Danzig, Stockholm, on the one side, and the towns along America's western coast on the other, will retain their original position in relation to the general level. As for Bermuda, the air just there will be as thin as it feels to aeronauts climbing as high as 8,000 metres up, as thin as on the highest summits of the Tibetan mountains, making life there quite impossible.

The same effect will apply for the diametrically opposite section, which includes the Indian Ocean, Australia and a quarter of the Pacific, which latter will in large part flood into the southern regions of Australia. There, the maximum point of displacement will be located along the Nuyts Land borders, and the cities of Adelaide and Melbourne will see the sea level drop to about eight kilometres below them. That the layer of air into which they will then be plunged will be of the purest, there is no doubt; but it will no longer be dense enough to support the requirements of breathing.

Such, broadly, are the changes that will affect areas in those two sections set to rise relative to emptied seabeds. Of course, new islands will appear there, formed by the peaks of submarine mountains in those regions not entirely drained of water.

However while the reduced thickness of breathable air layers will doubtless be unfortunate for those parts of continents raised into the upper reaches of the atmosphere, how will it be for those due to sink beneath incursions from the overflowing sea? It is still possible to breathe in air at less than atmospheric pressure. However, under even a few metres of water, breathing is impossible, and this is the situation that will confront those living in the other two sections.

In the section north-east of Kilimanjaro, the point of maximum effect will arrive at Yakutsk, in the middle of Siberia. From this town, submerged under 8,415m of water, less its original height above sea-level – the layer of liquid, thinning as it spread out, would extend right up to the section's demarcation lines, flooding the majority of Asiatic Russia and India, China, Japan, American Alaska to beyond the Bering Strait. Perhaps the Urals will still be visible, in the form of islets above the eastern stretch of Europe. As for St Petersburg and Moscow on the one side, and Calcutta, Bangkok, Saigon, Peking, Hong Kong and Edo on the other: these cities will vanish beneath a layer of water of variable depth, but quite sufficient to drown the Russians, Indians, Siamese, Cochin-Chinese, Chinese and Japanese, if they are not able to emigrate before disaster strikes.

In the section to the south-west of Kilimanjaro, the catastrophic effects will be less severe, because the majority of this section is covered by the Atlantic and Pacific, whose level will increase by 8,415M at its central point, the Falkland Islands. Nevertheless, vast land-masses are bound to disappear beneath this man-made deluge, among others the bulge of equatorial Africa, from Lower Guinea and Kilimanjaro down to the Cape of Good Hope and from that South American triangle formed by Peru, central Brazil, Chile and the Argentine Republic down to Tierra del Fuego and Cape Horn. The Patagonians, however tall they stand, will not escape submersion and will be unable even to take refuge up in that stretch of the Cordillera, for that range's southernmost peaks will not show at all in that part of the continent.

These then are the inevitable results – dropping below or hoisting above the new sea levels – produced by the re-levelling of the Earth's surface. Such are the contingencies for which those involved will have to prepare, if President Barbicane and his criminal operation are not prevented in time!

XVI

IN WHICH THE CHORUS OF UNHAPPY PEOPLE BOTH CRESCENDOES AND RINFORZANDOES

According to the Urgent Notice, it was imperative to address the perils of the situation, to out-manoeuvre or at least to avoid them, by travelling to the neutral lines where the risks would be minimal.

The threats to people fell into two categories: those facing asphyxiation and those facing drowning.

The Notice sparked a great range of reactions, most uniting in violent objection.

Among those facing asphyxiation were the North Americans, and the Europeans of France, England, Spain, etc. The prospect of acquiring new lands from the ocean floor was not sufficient to induce them to accept such changes. So Paris, relocated to a point roughly the same distance away from the new pole as she currently was from the old one, would not do well out of the move. The city would enjoy a perpetual springtime, it is true, but its layer of air would be substantially diminished. This was not the kind of news to have Parisians dancing in the streets, given their habit of extravagant oxygen consumption, in the absence of ozone … and this was just the beginning!

Among those to be drowned were the inhabitants of South America, also the Australians, Canadians, Indians and Zealanders. But would Great Britain suffer Barbicane & Co. to deprive her of her wealthiest colonies, where the Anglo-Saxon element has tended noticeably to take over from indigenous elements? It was inevitable that the Gulf of Mexico would be emptied, thereby forming a vast Antillean kingdom, to which both Mexicans and Americans might stake a claim in line with the Monroe Doctrine. Inevitable, too, that the basin containing the Sonde Islands, the Philippines and the Celebes Islands, once drained, would leave behind immense territories to which the English and Spanish might lay claim. But none of this would make up for the losses due to the terrible inundations.

If only the Samoyeds, or the Siberian Lapons, the Fuegans, Patagonians or even the Tartars, the Chinese, the Japanese or a few Argentinians could be the ones to disappear beneath the new seas, perhaps the civilized states might have accepted this sacrifice. But too many of the great powers were directly implicated in the disaster for them not to object.

As for Europe in particular, although her central regions would remain almost untouched, she would be lifted up along her western edge and pushed downwards to the east, which is to say, semi-asphyxiated on one side and half drowned on the other. Which was quite unacceptable. Moreover, the Mediterranean would be almost completely emptied, and this was something neither French, nor Italians, nor Spaniards, nor Greeks, nor Turks, nor the Egyptians would stand for, their position on that sea's shores conferring unarguable rights over its waters. Besides, what use would the Suez Canal be, despite being spared due to its location along a demarcation line? How to make use of M. de Lesseps' superb monument when there was no longer any Mediterranean on one side of the isthmus and hardly any Red Sea on the other? Short of extending the canal by a few hundred leagues…?

Whether England would consent to see Gibraltar, Malta and Cyprus turned into mountain peaks, lost in clouds, at which her warships would never again be able to dock, was an interesting question. She would surely not be satisfied by the territorial gains that would accrue to her in the former Atlantic basin. And yet, Major Donellan had already thought of returning to Europe to assert his country's rights over these new territories, in the event that Barbicane & Co.'s undertaking were a success.

In the light of all this, protests flooded in from around the world, even from those countries situated along the lines of zero re-levelling, for even they were somewhat affected in other ways. These protests grew yet more furious when the contents of the Zanzibar dispatch were revealed, revealing the position of the cannon and leading to the Urgent Notice above, which was hardly reassuring.

In short, President Barbicane, Captain Nicholl and J-T Maston were rejected by all humanity.

And yet, what fat times for newspapers of all shades! What demand for copies! What additional printings! It was perhaps the first time ever that papers generally in disagreement on all other questions were united in a single cause – from every nation's most important and most authoritative newspaper right down to the *MacLane Express*, an English newspaper concerned with economics, which anticipated widespread famine throughout the affected regions. It was not just the stability of Europe at risk of breakdown, it was the stability of the whole world. We may imagine the effect, therefore, on a world driven to desperation, in which the extreme anxiety such as characterized it towards the end of the nineteenth century made it vulnerable to every mad idea, to every crisis. It was a bomb dropped on a powder keg.

As for J-T Maston, you might have thought his last hour had come.

Indeed, on the evening of 17th September, a demented crowd broke into his prison intending to lynch him, and it has to be said, the police put up no opposition…

J-T Maston's cell was empty. By careful distribution of the worthy artillery-man's weight in gold, Mrs Evangelina Scorbitt had managed to engineer his escape. The guard's help was facilitated by the promise of a fortune that he fully intended to enjoy into his dotage, since, like Washington, New York and the other principal east coast cities, Baltimore was in the category of those that would be forced upwards, but where enough air would remain for the daily requirements of their inhabitants.

J-T Maston had clearly reached some mysterious refuge and so eluded an enraged public. Thus the life of this great troublemaker to the Old and New Worlds was saved by the devotion of a loving woman. And now, there were only four days to wait – four days! – before the projects of Barbicane & Co. would become a done deal.

The Urgent Notice had been as widely read as could be hoped. If there had at first been some scepticism regarding the predicted disasters, none now remained. Governments had hastened to warn those of their nationals – relatively small numbers of people – who were to be raised into zones of rarefied air; then those, of whom there were greater numbers, whose land would be engulfed by the seas.

Due to these warnings, conveyed by telegrams to all four corners of the Earth, there began a mass migration such as had never been seen before. Every race was represented, white, black, brown, yellow, etc., in one chromatic procession.

Unfortunately, time was running out. The hours were numbered. With a few months' breathing space, the Chinese could have left China, the Australians, Australia, the

Patagonians, Patagonia, the Siberians, the provinces of Siberia, etc. etc.

However, since the dangers were localised, now that it was known which places would be relatively unscathed, the terror itself grew more specific. Some provinces, even some states, began to feel reassured. Apart from in those regions that were directly threatened, there remained only the entirely natural apprehension of people awaiting a dreadful shock when the cannon was fired.

In the meantime, Alcide Pierdeux asked himself over and over, gesticulating like an old-fashioned telegraph tower: 'But how the Devil will President Barbicane manage to build a cannon a million times bigger than the twenty-seven? That Diabolical Maston! I would dearly like to meet him and set this tricky question to him face to face! It doesn't tally with any kind of sense, with anything rational, indeed it's a deal too much like a slingshot for words!'

However it appeared, the failure of the operation was in fact the sole chance remaining for parts of the planet to avoid wholesale disaster.

XVII

WHAT HAPPENED AT KILIMANJARO
OVER EIGHT MONTHS OF THIS
MEMORABLE YEAR

The Wamasai region lies to the east of central Africa, between the Zanzibar coast and the Great Lakes, where the Victoria Nyanza and the Tanganyika form so many inland seas. If a little is known about it, that's because the Englishman Johnston, Count Tekeli and the German Doctor Meyer all travelled through it. This mountainous country is ruled by the Sultan Bali-Bali, whose people consist of thirty to forty thousand negroes.

Three degrees south of the equator rise the Kilimanjaro highlands, whose tallest peaks – such as that of Kibo, among others – rise to a height of 5,704m. To its south, north and west, this substantial massif overlooks the vast and fertile plains of the Wamasai as it rolls out as far as Victoria Nyanza Lake, through lands belonging to Mozambique.

Several leagues short of Kilimanjaro's foothills lies the small town of Kisongo, the Sultan's usual residence. In fact, this capital is no more than a large village. It is populated by a very talented, very intelligent people, who work as much for themselves as by means of slaves, but all subject to the iron rule imposed by Bali-Bali.

The sultan is justly recognized as one of the most unusual of these central African tribal sovereigns who are trying to avoid the English influence or, more precisely, their control.

It was to Kisongo that President Barbicane and Captain Nicholl came, accompanied only by ten foremen devoted to their enterprise, in the first week of January.

On leaving the United States – a departure of which only Mrs Evangelina Scorbitt and J-T Maston were aware – they had set sail from New York for the Cape of Good Hope, from where another vessel carried them to the island of Zanzibar. From there a secretly loaded sloop carried them to the port of Mombasa on the African coast, the far side of the channel. An escort sent by the Sultan awaited them at this port and, after a difficult journey of some hundred leagues through this rugged country, thick with forests, riddled with rivers and peppered with swamps, they arrived at the royal residence.

On learning the results of J-T Maston's calculations, President Barbicane had made contact with Bali-Bali straight away, thanks to the mediation of a Swedish explorer who had just spent several years in that part of Africa. As one of President Barbicane's most fervent champions since the latter's famous voyage around the Moon – news of which had reached even to these distant lands – the sultan had conceived an affection for the daring American. Without divulging his purpose, Impey Barbicane had easily obtained the Wamasai ruler's authorization to undertake considerable building works along the southern side of Kilimanjaro. In return for a significant sum, equivalent to $300,000, Bali-Bali had agreed to provide him with all the assistance he required. What is more, he authorized Barbicane to do what he would with Kilimanjaro. He could treat the enormous volcanic mass according to his fancy: raze it to the ground, should he feel like it; carry it away, should he find the means. Following some very serious undertakings, out of which the Sultan did personally very well indeed, the North Polar Exploitation Association became proprietor of the African mountain just as it was of the Arctic territory.

President Barbicane and his colleagues were warmly welcomed in Kisongo. Bali-Bali felt an admiration verging on adoration for the two illustrious travellers who had launched themselves into space in order to reach the moon. Moreover, he had felt a special sympathy for the instigators of the mysterious undertakings that were approaching completion within his kingdom. In view of this he promised the Americans absolute secrecy – as much on his own part as on that of his subjects, whose assistance was assured. Not one of the negroes working at the site was allowed even a single day's leave, under pain of the most refined torture.

This is how the operation came to be wrapped in a secrecy that even the wiliest of American and European agents were unable to penetrate. The secret's eventual discovery was due to the sultan's relaxing his strictness following completion of the works; also because there are always traitors and gossips – even among negroes. Thus it was that Richard W. Trust, the consul of Zanzibar, caught wind of what was going on at Kilimanjaro. But by then, on 13th September, it was too late to stop President Barbicane from completing his work.

But why had Barbicane & Co. chosen the Wamasai as the theatre for their operation? First, the land was suitable due to its location in that little-known region of Africa and to its distance from regions more heavily frequented by travellers. Then, the Kilimanjaro massif provided all the qualities of solidity and orientation demanded by the project. What's more, all the primary materials required for the works could be found at the surface of this land, and in ideal conditions for their extraction.

Indeed, a few months before leaving the United States, the Swedish explorer had informed President Barbicane that iron and coal were abundantly available there right at the surface of the soil. No mines to dig, no seams to seek out thousands of feet down in the Earth's crust. They had only to dig at their feet to strike iron and coal, and in quantities clearly greater than their predicted needs. Moreover, also in the vicinity of the mountain, there were vast deposits of sodium nitrate and iron pyrite, both required for the production of the dyna-mix.

President Barbicane and Captain Nicholl had brought nobody else with them, apart from the ten foremen, whom they trusted absolutely. These men were to direct the ten thousand negroes Bali-Bali had put at their disposal, to whom now fell the task of building the monster cannon and its no less monstrous projectile.

Two weeks after President Barbicane and his colleague's arrival in the Wamasai, three enormous worksites had been established along Kilimanjaro's southern base, one for casting the cannon, another for casting the projectile, a third for the production of the dyna-mix.

Of course, casting a cannon of such colossal dimensions was a very demanding task. Indeed, the technical difficulty of completing it might have been the last chance of salvation for the peoples of the Old and New Worlds.

To cast a cannon of a million times greater volume than the standard 27 cm was actually beyond human capabilities. Already we struggle to build pieces of forty-two cm that can launch 780kg projectiles with 274kg of gunpowder. In view of this, Barbicane and Nicholl had not even considered attempting such a thing. It was not a cannon, nor even a shell, that they planned to build, but quite simply a tunnel bored into the solid massif of Kilimanjaro, a mineshaft, if you like.

Naturally, this mineshaft could stand in for the frame of the metal cannon, a gigantic *Columbiad* whose construction was as costly as it was difficult, and whose walls had to be of an inconceivable thickness, to prevent any chance of explosion. Barbicane & Co. had always planned to work in this way and, if J-T Maston's notebook talked about a cannon, that was because the twenty-seven had provided the model for his calculations.

Therefore, a site was picked out by eye about a hundred feet up on the southern slope of the mountain, below which the plains stretch out to the horizon. There could be nothing in the projectile's path when it was shot from the shaft sunk deep into the Kilimanjaro massif.

It was, then, with extreme precision and also a lot of sweaty work, that this shaft was dug. But Barbicane was easily able to furnish drills, which are relatively simple machines, and to operate them using air compressed by the mountain's many powerful waterfalls. Next, the holes pierced by the armies of drills were plugged with dyna-mix. This violent explosive was all that was needed to shatter the rock, for it was a type of extremely hard syenite, made up of orthose feldspar and amphibolic hornblende.

The thousands of labourers, led by the ten foremen, under the overall leadership of President Barbicane, applied themselves with such zeal and such intelligence that the works were completed in less than six months.

The tunnel measured twenty-seven metres in diameter against six hundred metres in depth. Since it was vital that the projectile should slide along an utterly smooth surface, without wasting any of the gas given off in the explosion, the tunnel's interior was lined with perfectly soldered cladding.

All this work was much more substantial than that which had been required by the celebrated *Columbiad* of Moon City, which had sent its aluminium projectile around the Moon.

While the slope of Kilimanjaro was being drilled, the labourers were not being idle at the second worksite. At the same time as the metal carapace was being built, they were busy constructing the vast projectile.

For this task, they had to obtain a cylindro-conical mass of pig iron weighing 180 million kilograms, that is 180 thousand tonnes.

Of course, it had never been the plan to cast this projectile from a single piece of metal. It was rather to be made up of thousand-tonne sections, to be successively hauled up to the tunnel's mouth and laid down in the chamber where the dyna-mix had already been packed. Once bolted together, these sections would form a compact whole, to slide as one along the tunnel's lined interior.

It was therefore necessary to supply the second worksite with roughly 400,000 tonnes of iron ore, 70,000 tonnes of limestone and 400,000 tonnes of bituminous coal, to be first turned into 280,000 tonnes of coke in the ovens. As the deposits of both lay close to Kilimanjaro, simple carts were sufficient to transport these supplies.

As for the construction of the great furnaces to smelt the ore, this caused perhaps the greatest difficulties. Nevertheless, after a month, ten vast furnaces, each thirty metres high, were standing by, each one capable of producing 180 tonnes per day. That would make 1,800 tonnes every twenty-four hours and 180,000 after a hundred days' non-stop production.

And as for the third worksite, where the dyna-mix was to be made, this work was easily done and in conditions of such secrecy that the composition of this explosive have still not been conclusively determined.

Everything had gone according to plan. Better progress could not have been achieved in any of the factories of Creusot, Cail, Indret, Seyne, Birkenhead, Woolwich or

Cockerill. And the accident rate was negligible, lower than for the average 300,000 Franc contract.

The sultan was delighted. He followed the works with untiring fascination. And the presence of their formidable monarch stimulated the zeal of his loyal subjects.

Occasionally, Bali-Bali would enquire what all this work was for:

'It is a project that will change the face of the world!' President Barbicane would reply.

'A great work,' added Captain Nicholl, 'that will guarantee Sultan Bali-Bali a greater, more enduring glory than all the other kings of Eastern Africa!'

The sultan could be seen quivering with pride as ruler of the Wamasai, and there was no need to press the point.

By 29th August, the works were entirely finished. Drilled to the desired calibre, the tunnel was sheathed in its smooth cladding for a distance of 600m. At the bottom, 2,000 tonnes of dyna-mix had been packed, with a fuse leading out to the keg of fulminate. Then came the 500m-long projectile. If the space taken up by the powder and the projectile were subtracted, there still remained 492m between the latter and the tunnel's mouth, to ensure the projectile's most effective deployment under the pressure produced by the expanding gases.

All this considered, the question arose – a question of pure ballistics: could the projectile deviate from the trajectory assigned to it by J-T Maston's calculations? Not an inch. The calculations were correct. They showed the degree by which the projectile's path must curve to the East of the Kilimanjaro meridian, due to the Earth's rotation on its axis, and also showed the shape of the hyperbolic curve that it would make due to its enormous initial speed.

A second question: would the projectile be visible during its flight? No, for, once beyond the tunnel and plunged into the Earth's shadow, it would be hidden from sight and besides, due to its low altitude, it would have considerable velocity. Once back in daylight, its slender shape would conceal it from the most powerful telescopes, and that all the more when, having shot free of the bonds of earthly gravity, it would move into eternal orbit around the Sun.

President Barbicane and Captain Nicholl could be truly proud of the operation they had thus brought so close to completion.

All that was missing was the presence of J-T Maston to admire the undertaking's skilful execution, worthy of the precision in calculation that had enabled it... More than anything, why should he be far away, very far – too far – when this awe-inspiring detonation was about to waken echoes as far as the furthest shores of Africa?

Thinking of Maston, his two colleagues had no doubt that he would have had to flee Ballistic Cottage, after escaping from the Baltimore jail, and that he would have gone into hiding for the sake of preserving his life. They had no idea of the extent to which public opinion had turned against the engineers of the North Polar Exploitation Association. They hadn't a clue that they would have been massacred, torn limb from limb, burned alive on slow fires had it been physically possible to lay hands on them. They were extremely lucky that, at the point when the shot would be fired, the only yells to greet them would be the cheers of an east African tribe.

'At last!' exclaimed Captain Nicholl to President Barbicane when, on the evening of 22nd September, they were relaxing together, admiring their masterpiece.

'Yes... at last!' replied Impey Barbicane, giving a sigh of relief.

'If we had to start all over again…'

'Then we would start over again!'

'What good luck,' remarked Captain Nicholl, 'that we were able to deploy our gorgeous dyna-mix!'

'That alone will be the making of your fame, Nicholl!'

'Naturally, Barbicane,' replied Captain Nicholl, modestly. 'But do you know how many tunnels we should have had to dig into Kilimanjaro to get the same result, if we'd had only gun cotton, as we did to launch our missile to the Moon?'

'Tell me, Nicholl.'

'180 tunnels, Barbicane!'

'Indeed! Then we would have dug them, Captain!'

'And 180 projectiles of 180,000 tonnes!'

'We would have cast them all, Nicholl!'

How to make men of such calibre see reason! But then, when a pair of gunmen have travelled right around the Moon, what on Earth could be beyond them?

But that very evening, only a few hours before the very minute intended for firing the shot, while President Barbicane and Captain Nicholl were thus congratulating each other, hidden away at his desk in Baltimore, Alcide Pierdeux gave a shriek like a redskin on the warpath. Rising abruptly from the table, which was buried in pages covered with scribbled algebraic formulae, he yelled:

'Maston you rogue! … Ah, the dog! How he's had me sweating my brains out over his equations! … How did I not see it sooner! Very devil of a cosine? … If I knew where he was right now I'd invite him to supper and have him join me in a champagne toast at the very second that his all-powerful, world-destroying creation is set to honk its horn!'

And, with another of those barbaric ululations with which he liked to spice up his games of whist:

'The old crackpot! He must have been up to his gills in gunpowder when he did the numbers for the cannon of Kilimanjaro! … He could have done with planning for quite a few more… though this was to be the *sine qua non* condition – or *sine cannon*, as we'd say back at the Ecole!'

XVIII

IN WHICH THE PEOPLE OF THE WAMASAI AWAIT PRESIDENT BARBICANE'S COMMAND FOR CAPTAIN NICHOLL TO 'FIRE!'

It was the evening of 22nd September – that memorable date to which public opinion assigned as unlucky a significance as that of 1st January of the year 1000.

Twelve hours after the Sun's passage over the meridian at Kilimanjaro, that is, at midnight, the terrible machine was due to be fired by the hand of Captain Nicholl.

We should mention here that, Kilimanjaro being 35 degrees to the east of the Paris meridian and Baltimore 79 degrees to the west of the that meridian, there was a difference of 114 degrees between the two places, which is equal to 456 minutes of time or seven hours and twenty-six minutes. Therefore, at the exact moment when the shot would be fired, it would be five hours and twenty-five minutes after midday in the great town of Maryland.

The weather was magnificent. The sun had just set on the Wamasai plains behind a perfect horizon, clear in every direction. You could not wish for a finer night, nor a quieter or more starry one, for launching a projectile into space. There wasn't a cloud to mingle with the artificial gases given off by the exploding dyna-mix.

Who knows? Perhaps President Barbicane and Captain Nicholl were sorry not to take their seats inside the projectile once more. Within the first second of flight they would have travelled 2,800 kilometres. Having already broached the mysteries of the lunar world, they might have delved into those of the solar one, and in much more interesting circumstances than the Frenchman Hector Servadac, who was carried off seated on the comet Gallia!*

Sultan Bali-Bali, along with the most important people in his court, his finance minister and his minister for great works, followed by the assistants who had contributed to the huge project, had all come together to watch every moment of the cannon's firing. However, as a precaution, everyone was positioned three kilometres away from the tunnel's mouth in Kilimanjaro, so as to have nothing to fear from the alarming eruption set to occur inside it.

All around, several thousand natives from Kisongo and other nearby towns to the south of the province had rushed – upon orders from Sultan Bali-Bali – to come and admire the sublime spectacle.

Wires connecting the fulminate detonator at the bottom of the tunnel to an electric battery were set up and ready to carry the current that would light the fuse and trigger the explosion of the dyna-mix.

As a prelude to the show, an excellent dinner brought the sultan, his American guests and all the worthies of his state together at the same table – at the sole expense of Bali-Bali, whose entertaining was all the more lavish in the knowledge that the cost would be reimbursed by the treasury of Barbicane & Co.

It was eleven o'clock when the banquet, begun at half past seven, concluded with the Sultan's raising a toast to the engineers of the North Polar Exploitation Association and to the success of their enterprise.

* See *Hector Servadac*, by the same author. [English translation of this title is 'Off on a Comet']

One more hour and the alteration in the Earth's geographical and climatological conditions would be a fait accompli.

President Barbicane, his colleague and the ten foremen now came to stand in a circle around the cabin housing the electric battery.

Barbicane, his chronometer in hand, was counting down the minutes – never had they seemed so long – the kind of minutes that feel, not like years but like centuries.

At ten to midnight, he and Captain Nicholl advanced towards the apparatus that was linked to the Kilimanjaro tunnel by its electric wire.

The sultan, his courtiers, the mass of natives, formed an immense circle around them.

It was essential that the shot be fired at precisely the moment designated by J-T Maston's calculations; that is, at the moment the sun crossed the equinoctial line – from which it would never stray again, once in its new orbit around the planet.

Five minutes to midnight! – Four minutes! – Three minutes! – Two! – One! …

President Barbicane was staring at his watch-hand, lit by a lantern held by one of the foremen, while, his finger resting on the machine's red button, Captain Nicholl stood ready to complete the electric circuit.

Twenty seconds to go! – Ten to go! – Five! – One! …

Not the slightest tremor was visible in the hand of the nerveless Nicholl. He and his colleague were no more anxious than when they had waited, sitting in their missile, for the *Columbiad* to shoot them up to the lunar realm!

'Fire!' cried President Barbicane.

And Captain Nicholl's index depressed the button.

A dreadful bang, whose thunderous rolls echoed out to the frontiers of Wamasai country. The high-pitched whistling of a great mass perforating the atmosphere under the pressure of thousands upon thousands of litres of gas forced out by the instantaneous explosion of 2,000 tonnes of dyna-mix. It was as if one of those meteors in which all of nature's violence seems pent up was passing close to the Earth's surface. And the effect could not have been more terrifying, even had all the cannons of all the artilleries in the world been combined with all the lightning the skies could muster and thundered away together.

XIX

IN WHICH J-T MASTON LOOKS BACK
RATHER FONDLY ON THE TIME WHEN
THE MOB WAS OUT TO LYNCH HIM

The capitals of both Old and New Worlds, and all their other sizeable cities, right down to every one of the humbler settlements, held their breath in deepest horror. Thanks to the profusion of newspapers distributed everywhere on the planet, every person knew the exact time at home that would correspond to midnight at Kilimanjaro, located as it was thirty-five degrees east, according to the longitudinal difference.

To mention only the principal cities – the sun travelling one degree for every four minutes – it was:

9.40 pm	in Paris
11.31 pm	in St Petersburg
9.30 pm	in London
10.20 pm	in Rome
9.15 pm	in Madrid
11.20 pm	in Berlin
11.26 pm	in Constantinople
3.04 am	in Calcutta
5.05 am	in Nanking

In Baltimore, as we have said, twelve hours after the Sun's passage over the Kilimanjaro meridian, it was 5.24 in the evening.

There is no need to dwell on the agonies experienced at this moment. The most talented of modern writers could not describe them – even by borrowing the style of the decadent or aestheticist school.

Baltimore's inhabitants knew they were in no danger of being swept away by the tidal wave of displaced seas, so all that lay in store for them was watching Chesapeake Bay run dry and Cape Hatteras, the bay's southernmost point, rise up like a mountain peak above the dried-up basin of the Atlantic. But, like so many others not directly threatened with emergence or submergence, there was a concern that the town might be knocked to pieces by the impact, her monuments destroyed, her districts swallowed down to the bottom of abysses that might suddenly gape along the Earth's surface. And these fears were, perhaps, equally justified in the various parts of the world not immediately to be swamped by the flux of displaced seas

Thus it was that every human creature felt a shiver of horror run through the very marrow of their bones during that fatal night. All were trembling – except one: the engineer Alcide Pierdeux. Having no time to broadcast his latest discoveries, he was sipping a glass of champagne in one of the best bars in the city, toasting the health of the Old World.

The twenty-fourth minute after five o'clock, corresponding to midnight at Kilimanjaro, ticked by…

In Baltimore… nothing!

In London, Paris, Rome, Constantinople, Berlin, nothing!… Not the least little bump!

Mr John Milne, observing the seismograph installed at the Takoshima coal mine in Japan, noted not the slightest abnormal movement in the Earth's crust in that part of the world.

And back in Baltimore, still nothing. Besides, the sky there was cloudy and so, after nightfall, it was impossible to know if the stars were beginning to modify their visible movement – which would have indicated a change in the Earth's axis.

What a night J-T Maston spent in his retreat, unknown to all save Mrs Evangelina Scorbitt. He was agitated, the fiery artillery-man. He could not stand still. He longed to be a few days older so he could see if the sun's passage had changed – an unarguable proof of the operation's success. Indeed, this change could first have been observed on the morning of 23rd September, for on that date the morning star always rises in the East, as seen from every point on the planet.

But… the next morning, the Sun appeared on the horizon just as it was wont to do.

At the time, the European delegates were gathered on their hotel terrace. They had assembled extremely precise instruments to enable them to say if today's Sun was travelling strictly along the equatorial plane.

Now, they detected nothing of the sort; a few minutes after rising, the radiant disk was already slipping towards the southern hemisphere.

Nothing about its path appeared to have changed.

Major Donellan and his colleagues greeted the celestial firebrand with heartfelt hurrahs and gave it a grand *entrée*, as they say in the theatre. It was a superb sky just then, the horizon just clear of the night's vapours; never had the great actor strode out to a lovelier scene, in such state of splendour and before such a delighted audience!

'And in the very spot fixed by the laws of astronomy!' exclaimed Eric Baldenak.

'Of our former astronomy,' observed Boris Karkof, 'that these lunatics were trying to destroy!'

'They'll be footing the bill for both the expense and the embarrassment!' added Jacques Jansen, through whom all Holland seemed to be speaking.

'And the Arctic shall remain eternally beneath its icy mantle!' exclaimed Professor Jan Harald.

'Hurrah for the Sun!' shouted Major Donellan. 'As he is, so he shall do for all the world's needs!'

'Hurrah! … Hurrah!…' repeated all the representatives of old Europe with one voice.

It was then that Dean Toodrink, who had said nothing until now, spoke up with this rather wise observation:

'But perhaps they never fired the shot?'

'Not fired?' expostulated the Major. 'Thank Heaven, rather, that they did fire, and twice instead of once!'

And that is exactly what J-T Maston and Mrs Evangelina Scorbitt were saying. It is also what both wise and ignorant were saying, for once united by the logic of the situation.

It is even what Alcide Pierdeux was saying to himself, though he added:

'Who cares whether they fired or not! The Earth has not stopped dancing upon her old axis and riding along just as she always has!'

In short, no one knew what had happened on Kilimanjaro. However, by the day's end, the question being asked by all of humanity had its reply.

A dispatch arrived in the United States, sent by Richard W. Trust of the consulate in Zanzibar, and this is what it said:

Zanzibar, 23rd September
Seven twenty-seven in the morning.
To John S. Wright, Minister of State
Shot fired yesterday evening midnight exactly from tunnel dug in Kilimanjaro south slope. Projectile flew with horrendous whistling. Terrifying explosion. Region devastated by whirlwind. Sea-level up as far as Mozambique Channel.

Many ships in distress and cast ashore. Towns and villages annihilated. All well.'
RICHARD W. TRUST

Indeed, all was well, for nothing about the basic situation had changed, except for the disasters experienced in the Wamasai, which was partly flattened by the man-made whirlwind, and the shipwrecks caused by atmospheric displacement – the same after-effects when the famous *Columbiad* had sent its projectile up to the Moon. Then, the shock, produced in Florida, had been felt for a radius of a hundred miles around. But this time, the effect ought to have been multiplied a hundred times.

Two important things of interest to the Old and the New World could be inferred from the dispatch:

1. That the enormous machine had been built within the very slopes of Kilimanjaro.
2. That the shot had been fired at the intended hour.

At this, the whole world gave a great shout of relief, which was followed by a great burst of laughter.

Barbicane & Co.'s great experiment had been a pitiful failure. J-T Maston's calculations were good for nothing but lighting fires. All that remained for the North Polar Exploitation Association to do was to declare bankruptcy.

Could it actually be that the Gun Club's secretary had made a mistake in his calculations?

'I should sooner believe myself mistaken in the affection he inspires in me!' thought Mrs Evangelina Scorbitt.

And out of everybody on Earth, the most downcast then living on the surface of the planet was indeed J-T Maston.

Seeing that the conditions under which the Earth spun around had not changed at all, he had held on to the hope that some incident had delayed his colleagues' execution…

But after the dispatch from Zanzibar, he was forced to acknowledge that the operation had failed.

Failed! … But what of the equations, the formulae by which he had calculated the operation's success? Was it that a gun six metres in length, twenty-seven wide, shooting a projectile of 180 million kilograms due to the explosion of 2,000 tonnes of dyna-mix at an initial velocity of 2,800 km was insufficient to cause the poles' displacement? No! That was impossible!

And yet…

Prey to a feverish excitement, J-T Maston declared that he intended to come out of hiding. Mrs Evangelina Scorbitt tried in vain to prevent him. Not that she feared for his life now, for the danger was over. But the mockery that would be directed at the unfortunate mathematician, the gibes that would flow unimpeded, the sarcasm that would rain down on his work – she would have liked to spare him these.

Worse, what welcome could he expect from his colleagues at the Gun Club? Would they not lay at his door the fiasco now covering them with ridicule? Was it not he, the author of the calculations, who must shoulder the entire responsibility for this failure?

J-T Maston would have none of it. He resisted Mrs Evangelina Scorbitt's pleading as he did her tears. He left the house where he had been hiding. He went out into the streets of Baltimore. He was recognized, and those whose livelihoods and very lives he had threatened, whose terror he had augmented by his obstinate refusal to speak, took their revenge by scoffing at him, by jeering at him in a thousand different ways.

They were quite something, those American kids, they could show the Paris street urchins a thing or two!

'Oy! Go on then, shift your axis will you!'

'Oy there, Mister Time-Maestro!'

'Oy! There goes the great No-Gun!'

Soon enough, the downcast, thoroughly castigated secretary of the Gun Club was obliged to retreat to the New Park mansion where Mrs Evangelina Scorbitt ran through her entire stock of comforting homilies as she tried to console him. In vain. J-T Maston would not be consoled, for his cannon had had no more effect on our planet than a 5th November rocket.

A fortnight went by like this and already the world, recovered from its terrors, was no longer concerned with the North Polar Exploitation Association's projects.

A fortnight, and no news of President Barbicane, nor of Captain Nicholl. Had they perished in the aftershocks of the explosion, during the havoc caused to the land of the Wamasai? Had they paid for the greatest enigma of modern times with their lives?

In fact, not.

After the shot was fired, both were knocked off their feet, along with the sultan, his court and several thousand natives, but they had got to their feet again, safe and sound.

'Has it worked?' asked Bali-Bali, rubbing his shoulder.

'Do you doubt it?'

'I… doubt? But when can you be certain?'

'In a few days!' replied President Barbicane.

If he had realized that the operation had been botched he would never have admitted it in front of the sovereign of the Wamasai.

Forty-eight hours later, the two colleagues had taken leave of Bali-Bali, not before paying a considerable sum as compensation for the disasters caused to the landscape of his kingdom. Since this sum went straight into the sultan's private coffers while his subjects saw not one dollar of it, His Majesty had no reason to regret this affair.

Then, followed by their foremen, the colleagues returned to Zanzibar, where they found a vessel bound for Suez. From there, the maritime post boat, the packet *Moeris*, carried them under false names to Marseille, the French national railway to Paris – without derailment or collision – the western trains to Le Havre, and finally the transatlantic liner *La Bourgogne* back to America.

In twenty-two days, they had travelled from the Wamasai to New York City, New York.

On 15th October, at three in the afternoon, they knocked at the door of the New Park mansion…

An instant later, they found themselves in the presence of Mrs Evangelina Scorbitt and J-T Maston.

XX

WHICH CONCLUDES THIS CURIOUS TALE, AS TRUE AS IT IS UNLIKELY

'Barbicane? Nicholl?…'

'Maston!'

'Is it you?'

'Yes, us!'

And in this pronoun, uttered simultaneously by the two colleagues in the same singular tone, could be heard a world of sarcasm and reproach.

J-T Maston rubbed his forehead with his iron hook. Then, in a voice that whistled from his lips – like the hiss of an asp, he said:

'Was the tunnel you dug into Kilimanjaro truly 600 metres long to a breadth of twenty-seven?' he asked.

'Yes!'

'The projectile did weigh 180 million kilograms?'

'Yes!'

'And the shot was indeed fired with 2,000 tonnes of dyna-mix?'

'Yes!'

The three yeses fell like bombs upon Maston's bowed head.

'In that case I conclude…' he went on.

'What?' asked President Barbicane.

'The following,' replied J-T Maston. 'Since the operation did not succeed, the powder can't have provided the projectile with the necessary initial velocity of 2,800 kilometres!'

'Really!' exclaimed Captain Nicholl.

'Your dyna-mix is good for nothing but water pistols!'

At this the captain jumped up, for he felt cruelly insulted.

'Maston!' he protested.

'Nicholl!'

'When you're ready to be blown up by dyna-mix, I'm sure…'

'No – with gun cotton! At least that's reliable!'

Mrs Evangelina Scorbitt had to intervene to calm the two irascible gunmen.

'Gentlemen! Gentlemen!' she cooed. 'We're all colleagues!'

At which President Barbicane spoke up more calmly:

'Why stoop to insults? Of course our friend Maston's calculations must be correct, just as we know that our friend Nicholl's explosive must be sufficiently powerful. Yes! We have put the very facts of science to the test! And yet, the experiment misfired. Why should that be? Perhaps we will never know?'

'In any case,' pronounced the Gun Club Secretary, 'we shall re-run it all again from the beginning!'

'What about all that money – spent entirely to no purpose!' remarked Captain Nicholl.

'And public sentiment,' added Mrs Evangelina Scorbitt, 'which will not allow you to risk destroying the Earth a second time.'

'What is to become of our Arctic kingdom?' shot back Captain Nicholl.

'How fast will shares in the North Polar Exploitation Association fall?' President Barbicane concluded sharply.

Meltdown! … But it had already happened; the shares were being sold for no more than the price of the old paper they were printed on.

Such was the end result of the whole enormous operation. Such was the memorable fiasco in which Barbicane & Co.'s superhuman project finished up.

If ever public ridicule was given free rein to shoot down decent if misdirected engineers; if ever the more wildly speculative newspaper articles, caricatures, songs and parodies found a rich seam to mine, we may confirm that it was indeed on this occasion. President Barbicane, the other administrators of the young society and their colleagues at the Gun Club, were booed. They were occasionally described with such… *gallic* abandon that the descriptions would not bear repeating in Latin – or even in Esperanto. Europe, particularly, abandoned all decorum with such a slew of sarcasm that the Americans were quite scandalized. And, lest we forget it: Barbicane, Nicholl and Maston were Americans, they belonged to that notorious Baltimore association, and they currently saw very little reason not to have the American government declare war on the entire Old World.

The last straw was a French ballad popularized by the distinguished singer Paulus (alive and kicking at the time). This ditty did the rounds of the café-concerts right around the world.

Here is one of the most popular verses:

> To fix up our grand old knick-knack
> Whose axis had all gone to rack
> They constructed a giant smokestack:
> The plan was to pack us some flak!
>
> That's enough to give you the jitters!
> Word goes out that we're after the critters,
> Three fools, after fame, all that glitters…
> Then all at once – crack!

The shot has been shot,
We're all here, nothing's not,
So: long live our great old knick-knack!

Would we ever know the cause of the operation's failure? Did the failure prove that the plan had been impossible to carry out; that the resources available to man will never be sufficient to cause a change in the Earth's diurnal movement; that the latitude of the Arctic Polar region can never be shifted such that the floes and icebergs might naturally be melted by the Sun's rays?

This was the topic of every conversation in the few days following President Barbicane and his colleague's return to the United States.

A simple note appeared in the *Temps* of 17th October, and M. Hébrard's paper enlightened the world on a point quite vital for its security.

The note ran as follows:

We know of the null result of the enterprise that had been aiming to bring about a new axis. However, since they are founded on correct facts, J-T Maston's calculations would have produced the desired result if, due to some inexplicable distraction, they had not been marred by error from the beginning.

The fact is, when the celebrated secretary of the Gun Club chose the circumference of the globe as his starting point, he took it to be 40,000 *metres* rather than 40,000 *kilometres* – which of course distorted his solution to the problem.

Whence could such an error come? Who could have caused it? How could such a brilliant mathematician have committed it? One is lost in vain conjecture.

What is clear is that, had the problem of shifting the axis been correctly framed, it ought to have been perfectly solved. But this early omission of three zeros produced an ultimate error of *twelve zeros* in the final calculation.

Rather than the one cannon a million times larger than the standard 'twenty-seven', there would have to be a trillion of these cannon, firing a trillion 180,000-tonne projectiles in order to shift the pole by 23°28, assuming that his dyna-mix has the explosive power Captain Nicholl accords it.

In short, the single shot, in the circumstances where it was fired from Kilimanjaro, only shifted the pole by three microns (three thousandths of a millimetre) and only modified the sea level to a maximum of nine millionths of a micron!

As for the projectile, a brand-new small planet, it belongs henceforth to our solar system, wherein it is held by solar gravity.

Alcide Pierdeux

So it was a moment's distraction on the part of J-T Maston, a three-zero error at the start of his calculations, that had produced such humiliation for the young society.

Yet, while his colleagues at the Gun Club made no secret of their fury, indeed cursing him roundly, the general public came out in support of the unfortunate man. After all, it was this error that had caused the whole fiasco – or rather the whole salvation, for it had saved the world from the most terrible calamities.

Millions of letters began to arrive from all over the world, every one a note of congratulation praising J-T Maston for his three-zero mistake.

All the more crushed, more downcast than ever, J-T Maston did his best not to hear the thunderous hurrah that the whole planet shouted in his honour. President Barbicane, Captain Nicholl, wooden-legged Tom Hunter, Colonel Bloomsberry, the dashing Bilsby and their colleagues would never forgive him…

At least he still had Mrs Evangelina Scorbitt. That excellent woman could not hold anything against him.

When he read Pierdeux's note, J-T Maston insisted on redoing his calculations, refusing to allow that he could have been so distracted.

And yet it was true. Pierdeux was not mistaken. That is why, having discovered the error at the very last minute, when there was no longer time to reassure his fellow creatures, the eccentric young man was able to be so perfectly calm amid the general frenzy. That is why he was raising a toast to the Old World at the very second the shot was fired from Kilimanjaro.

But *three zeros* left off the measurement of the Earth's circumference…?

At that point, J-T Maston suddenly remembered. It was at the very beginning of his work, when he had just shut himself away in his office in Ballistic Cottage. He had entirely accurately written out the number 40,000,000 on the blackboard…

Just then, a fervent ringing from the telephone. J-T Maston moves to the mouthpiece… He exchanges a few words with Mrs Evangelina Scorbitt… And then a thunderbolt sends both man and his blackboard for a tumble… He gets up… He starts to rewrite the number that has been half rubbed out in the fall… He has hardly shaped the digits 40,000… when the telephone rings a second time… And when at last he gets back to work, he forgets to replace the last three zeros in the figure for the Earth's circumference!

There it was. It was all Mrs Evangelina Scorbitt's fault. If she had not disturbed Maston, he might not have received that electric shock. Perhaps the thunderbolt would not have played such a sly, gallows-worthy trick on him, sufficient to compromise a lifetime of good, honest calculations.

And what a shock it was for the unhappy lady when J-T Maston was obliged to explain the circumstances that had led to the error. *She* was the cause of the disaster. It was her fault alone that J-T Maston would be dishonoured for all the long years remaining for him to live – for they generally died centenarians, in that venerable association the Gun Club.

Following that conversation, J-T Maston fled from the New Park mansion. He went back to Ballistic Cottage; he paced up and down his office, repeating to himself:

'I'm no good for anything at all, now!'

'Not even for marriage?' whispered a voice rendered heartbreaking by emotion.

It was Mrs Evangelina Scorbitt. Tearful, beside herself, she had followed Maston.

'Darling Maston!' she cried.

'Well – err – yes! But on one condition… that I shall never again practise mathematics!'

'Dearest, I hate mathematics!' replied the excellent widow.

And the secretary of the Gun Club made Mrs Evangelina Scorbitt into Mrs J-T Maston.

As for Alcide Pierdeux's note: what honour, what fame it brought to the engineer and, through him, also to his college. Translated into every language, republished in all the newspapers, that note carried his name around the whole world. It so happened, then, that the pretty Provençale girl's father, the same who had refused his daughter's hand in marriage because Pierdeux was 'much too learned', read the note in the *Petit Marseillais*. So it was that, on coming to understand the note's significance unaided by any external prompt, struck with remorse and in hope of a better outcome, he sent its author an invitation to dinner.

XXI

VERY SHORT BUT ENTIRELY
REASSURING AS TO
THE FUTURE OF OUR PLANET

From now on, let the Earth's inhabitants take heart. President Barbicane and Captain Nicholl would not re-attempt the enterprise that had so miserably gone up in smoke. J-T Maston would not redo his calculations, this time without error. It would have been pointless. The engineer Alcide Pierdeux's note was correct. As shown by the mechanics, producing a 23°28' displacement in the axis, even using dynamix, would require a trillion cannon like the one that had been tunnelled into the slopes of Kilimanjaro. Now, were the entire surface of our planet quite solid, it would still be too small to contain them all.

So it seems that the Earth's inhabitants may sleep easy in their beds. Modifying the conditions under which the Earth itself spins is beyond the power allotted to humankind; it is not for us to tinker with any aspect of the order established by the Creator for the smooth running of our Universe.

BIOGRAPHICAL NOTE

Jules Gabriel Verne was born in 1828 in Nantes, France. His father, Pierre, was a lawyer, and his mother, Sophie Allotte, came from a family of shipbuilders and sea captains. Verne's father intended that he should become a lawyer, but Verne refused to do anything but write. In 1848 he went to Paris, supposedly to study law, but in fact to further his literary career. There he met Victor Hugo and Alexandre Dumas, who encouraged him to write historical novels, a popular literary genre at that time. Verne disliked the historical novel, however, and set about writing articles, short stories and plays instead, one of which, *The Broken Straws*, was performed in 1850. That same year, Verne's father learned that his son had abandoned his studies and so discontinued his allowance; Verne was therefore forced to sell stories for a living.

After continuing to write for years with little success, in 1863 Verne wrote *Five Weeks in a Balloon*, the first of a successful cycle of sixty-three novels of adventure and fantasy. Initially refused for publication because it was considered too scientific and not sufficiently exciting or adventurous, it was finally published by a press that specialized in children's books. It was translated into many languages and Verne found that he had become both rich and famous.

Verne took an active interest in the latest scientific knowledge and current theories about the earth, and his works – *Journey to the Centre of the Earth* (1864), *From the Earth to the Moon* (1865), *20,000 Leagues Under the Sea* (1870) and *Around the World in Eighty Days* (1873) among them – reflected his passion, and have earned Verne the title of the founder of modern science fiction.

Verne died on 24th March 1905 in the city of Amiens.

Sophie Lewis is a London-born writer, editor and translator from French. Recent translations include *Thérèse and Isabelle* by Violette Leduc, for Salammbô Press, and *The Man Who Walked Through Wall*s by Marcel Aymé, for Pushkin Press. She is Editor-at-Large at And Other Stories press, and moved to Rio de Janeiro in 2011.

ACKNOWLEDGEMENTS

Thank you to Peter Stanton for general scientific sense, Sophie and Jean-Dominique Langlais for advice on quirks of Vernian language, and Ben Coates for essential guidance in mathematics. Equally important thanks to my readers: David Hermann, Pauline Le Goff and Harold Lewis.

– Sophie Lewis

HESPERUS PRESS

Hesperus Press is committed to bringing near what is far –
far both in space and time. Works written by the greatest
authors, and unjustly neglected or simply little known in
the English-speaking world, are made accessible through
new translations and a completely fresh editorial approach.
Through these classic works, the reader is introduced to the
greatest writers from all times and all cultures.

For more information on Hesperus Press, please visit our
website: **www.hesperuspress.com**

SELECTED TITLES FROM HESPERUS PRESS

Author	Title	Foreword writer
Pietro Aretino	*The School of Whoredom*	Paul Bailey
Pietro Aretino	*The Secret Life of Nuns*	
Jane Austen	*Lesley Castle*	Zoë Heller
Jane Austen	*Love and Friendship*	Fay Weldon
Honoré de Balzac	*Colonel Chabert*	A.N. Wilson
Charles Baudelaire	*On Wine and Hashish*	Margaret Drabble
Giovanni Boccaccio	*Life of Dante*	A.N. Wilson
Charlotte Brontë	*The Spell*	
Emily Brontë	*Poems of Solitude*	Helen Dunmore
Mikhail Bulgakov	*Fatal Eggs*	Doris Lessing
Mikhail Bulgakov	*The Heart of a Dog*	A.S. Byatt
Giacomo Casanova	*The Duel*	Tim Parks
Miguel de Cervantes	*The Dialogue of the Dogs*	Ben Okri
Geoffrey Chaucer	*The Parliament of Birds*	
Anton Chekhov	*The Story of a Nobody*	Louis de Bernières
Anton Chekhov	*Three Years*	William Fiennes
Wilkie Collins	*The Frozen Deep*	
Joseph Conrad	*Heart of Darkness*	A.N. Wilson
Joseph Conrad	*The Return*	Colm Tóibín
Gabriele D'Annunzio	*The Book of the Virgins*	Tim Parks
Dante Alighieri	*The Divine Comedy: Inferno*	
Dante Alighieri	*New Life*	Louis de Bernières
Daniel Defoe	*The King of Pirates*	Peter Ackroyd
Marquis de Sade	*Incest*	Janet Street-Porter
Charles Dickens	*The Haunted House*	Peter Ackroyd
Charles Dickens	*A House to Let*	
Fyodor Dostoevsky	*The Double*	Jeremy Dyson
Fyodor Dostoevsky	*Poor People*	Charlotte Hobson
Alexandre Dumas	*One Thousand and One Ghosts*	

George Eliot	*Amos Barton*	Matthew Sweet
Henry Fielding	*Jonathan Wild the Great*	Peter Ackroyd
F. Scott Fitzgerald	*The Popular Girl*	Helen Dunmore
Gustave Flaubert	*Memoirs of a Madman*	Germaine Greer
Ugo Foscolo	*Last Letters of Jacopo Ortis*	Valerio Massimo Manfredi
Elizabeth Gaskell	*Lois the Witch*	Jenny Uglow
Théophile Gautier	*The Jinx*	Gilbert Adair
André Gide	*Theseus*	
Johann Wolfgang von Goethe	*The Man of Fifty*	A.S. Byatt
Nikolai Gogol	*The Squabble*	Patrick McCabe
E.T.A. Hoffmann	*Mademoiselle de Scudéri*	Gilbert Adair
Victor Hugo	*The Last Day of a Condemned Man*	Libby Purves
Joris-Karl Huysmans	*With the Flow*	Simon Callow
Henry James	*In the Cage*	Libby Purves
Franz Kafka	*Metamorphosis*	Martin Jarvis
Franz Kafka	*The Trial*	Zadie Smith
John Keats	*Fugitive Poems*	Andrew Motion
Heinrich von Kleist	*The Marquise of O–*	Andrew Miller
Mikhail Lermontov	*A Hero of Our Time*	Doris Lessing
Nikolai Leskov	*Lady Macbeth of Mtsensk*	Gilbert Adair
Carlo Levi	*Words are Stones*	Anita Desai
Xavier de Maistre	*A Journey Around my Room*	Alain de Botton
André Malraux	*The Way of the Kings*	Rachel Seiffert
Katherine Mansfield	*Prelude*	William Boyd
Edgar Lee Masters	*Spoon River Anthology*	Shena Mackay
Guy de Maupassant	*Butterball*	Germaine Greer
Prosper Mérimée	*Carmen*	Philip Pullman
Sir Thomas More	*The History of King Richard III*	Sister Wendy Beckett
Sándor Petőfi	*John the Valiant*	George Szirtes